Trapped in the Mind-Zone

Indoosri

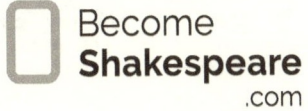
Become
Shakespeare
.com

First published in 2019 by

Becomeshakespeare.com

Wordit Content Design & Editing Services Pvt Ltd
Unit - 26, Building A -1, Nr Wadala RTO,
Wadala (East), Mumbai 400037, India
T: +91 8080226699

Wordit Art Fund helps deserving authors
publish their work by providing monetary support.
To apply for funding, please visit us at
www.BecomeShakespeare.com

©

ISBN - 978-93-88930-25-3

This book is a work of fiction. Names, characters, places and incidents
either are products of the author's imagination or are used fictitiously.
Any resemblance to actual events or locals or persons, living or dead,
is entirely coincidental.

To my sisters

Manju, Jaishree and Chitra

About the Author

I don't have fancy credential. I have travelled to some interesting places in life and in my mind. An Indian at heart and a global one at that. I do love to walk anywhere. Well...that's it!

Tell me what you feel about this story... just email at indoosri@gmail.com

CHAPTERS

1
The Beginnings

Gentle wind spiralled carrying a few scattered leaves in its spirals. It breezed through the roads, lanes, back lanes, in and out of houses, and finally homed down at a certain location where an unusual scene was unfolding.

It was a very quiet night, and thirteen year old Feroz could hear every little sound: the creak of the cupboard door, opening and closing in the mild breeze of the fan; the groaning and grunting of the old chair; the water dripping from the tap...tip...tip...tip. It did not bother him much; in fact he liked to listen to the perfect timing of each drop. The more he heard, the more aware he became of the other different sounds of the night. He felt restless and awake, he tossed and turned, but sleep evaded him. So he did what he loved doing under such circumstances 'count the different unique sounds'.

He lived in an area that was close to the Army cantonment in Delhi. His bungalow was the last one of the row of bungalows on Park Lane. So on the right side of his house was the colony of Park Lane and on the left side was the Army Cantt. His room was on the first floor of their duplex house. They had a kitchen garden on one side and a small garden on the other side. The garden was lined with thick bushes which doubled up as a natural fence. Beyond their garden, at an angle was one solitary bungalow that came under the Delhi cantonment board. Further ahead, the road then joined another road that led to Kirby Place.

Feroz concentrated; he felt he heard a strange unknown sound right outside his window, something like 'ssss...hissss'. He got up and parted the curtains just a little and peered outside. It was pitch black. He couldn't see anything, but he kept peering opening his eyes wide, and slowly his eyes got accustomed to the darkness, he could make out the outline of the familiar bushes in their backyard. He scanned the area, and his eyes stopped at a strange sight. He got goose bumps all over and suddenly felt chilly. There was a snake... a snake with its hood up, and right in front of it was a cat. It was a freaky sight. He realized it was the same cat that often strolled around in their garden; it was almost like a member of their house!

Ooooh.... will the snake eat the cat? Do snakes eat cats? He wasn't sure.

Suddenly as if by intuition both the creatures turned, and looked up at his window; he let go of the curtain, and stood still. He felt a little frightened. His heart was beating fast; he controlled the urge to look out again.

When the pace of his heart slowed down a bit, he again parted the curtain a little, certain that the snake would now be on his window.

That would be frightful, he imagined.

Gathering courage he looked out and saw that the cat was going into the bushes with the snake behind it. It became quiet and still again. He thought he saw a shadow flit by and roved his eyes on the bushes. There was nothing, still he watched silently. After quite a while, when nothing moved, he let go of the curtain and snuggled into his bed. He pondered about the scene that he had just witnessed and gradually sleep crept in.

'Feroz... Feroz... get up, beta you will be late for school,' his mother shook him awake.

He hauled himself from the bed and lumbered into the bathroom, leaning against the wall he snoozed for a few more minutes. Slowly the happenings of the strange night awakened him fully. He brushed his teeth hurriedly, and got ready as fast as he could. Before going to the bus stop, he ran behind his house to check if he could see any signs of the snake or the cat. He looked at the spot, there seemed to be nothing-- *no signs.*

Had he been dreaming? His Mom always said, 'Feroz you have an over active mind!!'

He thought he had a juicy tale to tell his friends but now he started feeling unsure about the whole incident.

Today he had Science class in the first two periods; he decided he would ask his Science Sir, Mr Batra whether snakes eat cats... that is if his Sir was in a good mood! They called him 'Prof Moody' because of his swinging moods and also after the famous character in the Harry Potter story.

He reached his school, and eagerly waited for the first period to start.

'Alright children,' said Batra Sir, 'today you are going to attend one of the most interesting science lessons of your life. I have taken special permission from the Principal to show you my pets, yes... I have several birds and animals as pets. During the course of this year I will be showing you some of my pets. Today, I have brought my favourite pet: his name is 'Specter'.

He opened a carton and took out a glass container, and in it was a long snake!! Feroz was taken aback. It looked exactly like the one he had seen last night. The whole class was excited, and was making a lot of noise, but all that Feroz could do was gape.

For Feroz the class passed in a daze. Sir explained everything about snakes: which were poisonous, which weren't; when they strike, when they rest, what they eat, what should be done when a snake bites, the first aid measures etc etc. In the end he said, 'Children, yesterday I took my snake out of the glass container to clean the container so that all of you can get a good look at Specter. While I was drying the container Specter vanished into thin air. I searched, and searched, but couldn't find it. I thought something terrible must have happened, it might have slipped out, and maybe got run over by a car. I searched everywhere till late in the evening, but couldn't find it. I gave up. At night while I was sleeping I heard my cat mewing and clattering. So I went to investigate, and what do you think I found -- Specter was right there inside the glass container. I was so happy to have Specter back, Phew!!'

He let out a sigh of relief and said, 'Ok, with this story, this class is over. All of you can go and play for the rest of the period while I go, and leave Specter back home.'

Feroz's overactive mind started ticking like a clock. Is it possible?

He started thinking whether he should tell his friends about the snake and the cat that he had seen.

His friend Ajay came and said, 'Feroz come out and play, what are you thinking about?'

Feroz said to himself *'Forget it, nobody will believe me!!'* And he went out to play with his friends.

The rest of the day in school was quite tough; they were made to study hard. All the teachers were really bent upon working the students and taught the chapters with lot of enthusiasm, questioning them and giving lengthy answers to questions. They had a lot of homework in nearly all the subjects.

By the time the school got over Feroz was really drained and did not talk to anybody in the bus. The heat added to his exhaustion, his eyes felt heavy. Sleep invaded his body, he tried hard not to sleep but his eyes kept closing. His neck turned into jelly and his head lolled this way and that way uncontrollably. He kept jerking himself awake and peeked left and right to see if anyone was watching him. Within seconds his eyes closed again and whole process continued till his bus stop arrived.

2
Shadowy Business

Feroz got off the school bus and immediately found the stone that he was going to kick all the way home. He gave it a kick and started walking. The sun was shining fiercely; he licked his lips several times, he liked it when the slight breeze brushed his moist lips. There was just a little, dry wind blowing and things were quiet on the road. It was that time of the day when there is a lull in all activities.

He pictured himself taking out a bottle of cold water from the fridge and gulping it. He actually felt the coolness spread through his body. He hurried faster kicking the stone harder, so that it would roll further. He saw the shadows of the telephone lines crisscrossing forming an interesting web. He decided to forget about the stone and walk on these shadows only. He chose one shadow and started walking on it, it crisscrossed several other shadows, but he kept following it. Wherever the lines crossed each other he picked the one that went towards his house. Jumping over all the obstacles that came on his way he reached home or rather a line of shadow reached his house.

He opened the gate with a loud clatter and pressed the bell a little bit longer than required, he knew his Mom would rush to open the door. He pushed the door and found that it was already open. His mother sometimes did that, the coolness of the house brought a wave of relief.

He rushed to the fridge and took out the coldest bottle of water and without bothering to pour the water in a glass he just put his mouth on the bottle and took a large gulp and another gulp and another, till the whole bottle was empty. Satisfied he went towards the kitchen, nobody was there, he checked the dishes kept ready for lunch, and the food looked yummy...he was ravenous.

'Mom' he yelled 'I am hungry.'

He returned to the living room put on the TV and kicked off his shoes and sprawled on the couch. He stopped surfing the channel when he saw a boy pointing at a display of mouth-watering array of ice creams and saying 'I will have Minty chocolate'

He must have fallen asleep at some point because when he woke up he was still in his uniform. He looked out and was surprised to find that it looked a little dark. He looked at the watch and saw that it was six in the evening, *had he slept through lunch?* He realized he had not had his lunch. His Mom had let him sleep through. *Unbelievable!* He went to his Mom's room and found that she wasn't there.

He rushed to all the rooms, and checked, no one was there. He got worried and started thinking, *Where is Mom? Perhaps she has gone to the market to get something? But she would never leave the house open like this. Maybe someone has kidnapped her, no... but then nothing looked stolen from the house, no sign of violence. Maybe she has gone to our neighbours' house across the road to get something and got hit by some vehicle and is now in the hospital.* His eyes pricked with tears when all these thoughts ravaged his mind.

What should I do now? He asked himself. Feeling confused and alarmed he pleaded god, Oh! God, please let my Mom be safe and sound. I will be a good boy; I'll do whatever she says. Please, please please ...

He quickly changed and picked up the phone to inquire from the neighbour. He stopped and thought *but... what will I ask? It would be better if I go and check,* and so he changed his mind and kept the phone back. He put on his shoes and locked the door and started to cross the road when a shadow darted across. He stopped, terrified. He spun on the spot and looked all around nothing unusual was there. He started to cross the road; from the corner of his eyes he saw the shadow again, it was following him! He started running and was soon at the door step of their neighbour. He gave the bell a push, just a short buzz this time.

Mrs Mahajan opened the door. Feroz wished her and inquired whether his mother had dropped by. Mrs Mahajan exclaimed 'Yes! But she left for the market and would have long got back. Isn't she home?'

Feroz didn't know what to say, he just turned around and ran away. *Funny boy!* Thought Mrs Mahajan and went inside.

Feroz ran wildly back home. On the way thinking, perhaps his Mom was back, perhaps she forgot to lock the door before going. He also started feeling guilty that he had slept off; he could have started this search long back. He saw his house was still in darkness; he went inside and rushed through all the rooms putting all the lights on... Empty. Empty. Empty and finally he checked his own room. He looked out of his window, the same shadow darted behind a tree, and he could partly see the shadow. A couple of Mynahs on a branch of the tree were looking intently at the shadow.

Feroz stood very still and quiet and very faintly he heard the shadow say 'Hey you, I got detached from my owner in the market place, I followed her, but am unable to get attached to her, help me please'.

Feroz was taken aback. *Was the shadow talking about his mother? Was it talking to him?* He was about to reveal himself to the shadow when he heard the Mynahs cackling. He peered out just in time to see the birds holding something dark and flying into the sky.

Oh! Have I let my mind wander again? He felt sad and unhappy and said aloud 'What is happening to me?'

'Feroz, Feroz! Come here' he heard.

Feroz stood transfixed for a few seconds...that was his mother's voice! He ran towards the kitchen from where he had heard the call come from and saw his Mom warming milk for him. Standing, as if, she had been there all along.

'Mom, where have you been?' He asked.

'What?' Mom said, 'Drink up this milk and why didn't you have the Minty chocolate ice cream that I brought for you? Really Feroz... I don't know what gets into you sometimes, you really tire me. I have to keep telling you to do this and that....,' and she went about doing her business mumbling.

Feroz went to his room trying to make some sense of all of it. If he said anything at all to his parents about this they would not believe him.

'Was his Mom at home all along? He said to himself, 'did I go to our neighbour's house? I can call and ask... No... Forget it, nobody will believe me! Mynahs carrying Mom's shadow, unbelievable....' He recalled the snake and the cat incident. A shadow had definitely darted, he was sure now. Something was happening he just couldn't pinpoint what exactly it was. He decided he would keep a close watch on that cat.

3
Yapra

Feroz woke up with a start the next day. He looked at his watch, there was still half an hour before his Mom would come and wake him up. He lazed around and rolled over trying to go back to sleep. After fifteen minutes of tossing and turning he decided to get up and get ready.

He entered the living room, looking smart in his uniform, hoping to watch some program on the TV.

'Oh, you are up and ready?' remarked his dad, who was having his morning tea and watching the news on the TV.

Feroz nodded and picked up his glass of milk and gulped it, spilling few drops on his school uniform. He saw his father looking disapprovingly at him. He kept the glass down and contemplated going to the bus stop, it was too early! He eyed the remote but did not dare to pick it up. He sat down on the couch and picked up the newspaper instead and searched for the cartoon strip.

'Don't slouch and sit straight, erect.'

Feroz pulled himself all the way up and stood and read the strip standing, just to bug his father. He was beginning to feel irritated. He got out of the house and walked slowly towards the school bus stop.

As he approached his bus stop he saw a man standing there. There were five street dogs lunging and snapping at him. Feroz eyed the dogs and stopped, afraid that they would turn on him. The man swiftly looked in his direction and then at the dogs. Instantly the dogs scattered away.

Feroz thought that was weird and he became alert. He looked furtively all around. Other than an old man walking way down the road, there was nobody else. He bent down to retie his shoe lace and sneaked a look at the man. The man was still looking at him; a chill ran through his spine. His hands trembled as he tied the shoe lace for the third time. When he got up he saw that the man had crossed the road and was walking towards a shack on the other side of the bus stop.

Feroz relaxed, he was unnecessarily getting worked up. There was still plenty of time, he looked towards the shack and had this uncontrollable urge to see what was inside the shack. He decided he would take just one peek through the window and come straight back to the bus stop.

He crossed the road and took a round about route to the back side of the shack. There was a broken window with no glass. With his back pressed tightly on the wall, he peeked in. It was surprisingly clean inside. There was a wall which had built-in cemented slots for keeping things. The top two shelves were completely filled with books, the third shelf was sparsely filled with neatly folded clothes and the last one was cluttered with plates, bowls, cups, bottles and all kinds of odds and ends. The doors were wide open and one side of the door was hanging on broken hinges. There were stray dogs lazing around. The man was sitting on a big flat rock with his back to the window. He was stroking and patting a huge dog. Abruptly, he put one hand behind his back and held out three fingers, the dog cocked its head and barked three times. The man held out one finger and the dog barked ones. Feroz was astonished, the man then held out four fingers and the dog barked four times. All of a sudden the man turned around and smiled at Feroz.

Feroz felt uneasy.

'Why don't you come through the door and watch?' The man said in perfect English.

Feroz shook his head and started running back to his stop. He heard the man yell, 'we will meet again when your partner joins you.'

Feroz hurried on, wondering what the crazy man meant by 'partner.'

Ajay saw Feroz running and coming from the opposite direction to his usual.

'How come you are coming from that side?' He asked pointing his thumb towards the road.

Feroz narrated his story. Bonty joined them in between and heard the story too.

'Let us go and meet this crazy-dog-man when we get back from school today,' Bonty suggested.

'Yes, yes...let's do that, we are your partners after all,' Ajay added with titters.

Feroz, Ajay, and Bonty were thick friends. In fact Feroz believed that they were friends from the moment they were born, He would tell anyone willing to listen 'We have been friends since we came to this earth.' Once he said that to Ajay's older sister and she gave him an exasperated look and said, 'You are a crazy boy! Feroz... what an odd statement that is... from the time we have been on earth,' she mimicked. He couldn't understand why she wouldn't believe him.

The school hours passed rather slowly, Feroz thought a lot about the man and the dog. He was eager for the school to get over and go with his friends to the shack.

Finally it got over and all three of them whispered excitedly on the bus about the crazy-dog-man.

When they got off the school bus, they waited till the other school children had left and then headed towards the shack. They reached the shack, the door was open. Nobody was there inside; they didn't enter the room, but just peered in. They were very disappointed that the man was not there. Feroz glanced at the broken door and noticed that something was etched on the wall. He went closer and tried to decipher what was written. A single word was written ~Yapra

'Yapra,' he mumbled, 'I think the man's name is Yapra.'

They crowded over the etching. Bonty cleaned the etching and now it shone clearly. He cleaned the wall some more... all around the word, nothing else was written.

The broken door suddenly swung on the hinges even though there was no breeze. The boys jumped a little. They looked inside, two dogs were dozing,

'Is one of these the dog?' Bonty asked whispering.

'Nope,' whispered Feroz, 'it was a huge one.'

They turned to leave and saw one of the dogs stir, open its eyes and gaze at them. They hastened their retreat, afraid that it would decide to bark or run after them.

They talked for some time and then they split up to go back home. Bonty and Ajay headed in one direction and Feroz in the other. Though they lived in the same colony Feroz's house was closer from the Cantt side, while his friends' houses were deeper inside the colony and hence closer from the other direction.

On the way Feroz noticed that there was some activity going on in the neighbouring empty bungalow. Somebody was moving in. He decided he would check out later in the evening.

'Yapra' mouthed Feroz as he walked towards his house and started thinking... *How was he doing that trick of making the dog bark exactly the number of times he wanted it to? Did Yapra know all along that I was standing and watching through the window? What did he mean by 'we will meet again when your partner joins you.'*

4
Collocation

Firan watched as the huge truck backed into their driveway. She was feisty girl, full of action and energy. Her dad was in the army and they kept moving every two years. For her, it was hard to imagine that their whole house was now inside this truck. Just about ten days back they had been packing all their belongings into the trunks. Her Mom had been discarding more than packing: old things, broken things, torn things, chipped things, faded things, unused things, and unwanted things were piled in one corner of the room -- a mini hill of give-aways!

Firan was allotted two trunks one for clothes and one for other items. She had stuffed them with everything that was dear to her whether torn or faded or broken, she wanted to take them all, and could not part with anything. So she stuffed her boxes as much as possible. She also managed to stuff some of her things in other trunks that were not hers!

The truck backed slowly; the driver ensuring not to hit the gate. Two men quickly started unloading; two other started carrying them inside the house. There was a flurry of people rushing in and out, shouting watch out... Dekh ke... Firan tried to stay out of the way. `Firan's trunks were dumped in a room that was hastily decided to be hers. She liked her room instantly it was nice, big, full of light and airy! It was on the first floor of the duplex house. It overlooked a part of their garden and the other window overlooked the backyard. She gazed out feeling very thrilled. Each time they moved and relocated she had this same feeling of excitement mixed with apprehension.

Will I find good friends? Will the school be just as good as the last one? Hope the teachers aren't strict and hope they don't give too much of homework and tests. All these thoughts bombarded her mind.

The next day all the trunks were scattered here and there in half empty state. Her parents were working in a frenzied manner setting up the house, deciding where to put what. Firan loved this part of unpacking - no rules, no proper routine and most importantly no school for her, while her classmates were slogging away at some school or the other. She wished this period would go on and on and on. She loitered around in the house, getting in everybody's way. She tried to be of some help, but it was hopeless, whatever she did seemed wrong, she broke a glass while unpacking, slipped and fell, misplaced items. Finally her Mom sent her to her own room and asked her to sort her own trunks out.

She heaved the lid of the trunk up and looked inside, everything looked so new. She had forgotten that she had these tattoos and stickers. She took the tattoos out and examined them. She treasured them and was saving them to put them on some special occasion. She saw her secret diary and got distracted, left the tattoos and took out her diary and opened the pages and read a few lines. Everything came out one by one: clothes, toys, posters, story books, ear rings, bangles, bags, shoes, water colours, dolls, and 'Gruffy' the huge stuffed dog that was tattered but had been with her since she was four. The room that had seemed huge when it was empty now looked small and cluttered.

Where am I going to put all these things? She thought helplessly, 'there is no place, this is where and when Mom comes in' she said to herself and conveniently scooted out.

She slipped out of the side door and into the garden. The garden was a bit overgrown and had a wild look, with bushes and shrubs growing everywhere. Dry leaves were scattered around and they were rustling in the breeze making a pleasant sound. Firan purposefully stepped on some leaves to hear the crushing sound. She parted some shrubs and pushed through them to see what was on the other side. She scrambled on her fours and peered into the neighbours' garden. Just at that very moment a face looked at her and she shrieked and screamed. 'The face' also shrieked and screamed. The deafening shrieks had everybody from both the houses running towards the shrubs.

'What happened? What happened?' shouted Firan's mother, adding to the commotion.

Her father came dashing towards her. On the other side two men and two women pushed through the foliage of trees, leaves and bushes, and peered along with the 'face'.

Everybody started laughing and getting introduced.

'Hello, we are your new neighbour,' said Firan's Mom.

'Hello,' said a man and a woman together on the other side.

'I am Dr Shah, this is my wife Reema and that's my son Feroz,' said Dr Shah pointing at 'the face'.

Oh! 'The face' has a name thought Firan wickedly.

'I am Col Amir, my wife Manu and this is Firan,' added Firan's dad.

'This is our gardener and our maid,' said Reema on the other side 'If you need any help, please don't hesitate to ask.'

After exchanging a few niceties and a promise to meet later everybody dispersed. Firan glared at Feroz before turning her back.

Firan felt that all boys were crass; she got into quite a few fights with them in her old school. She had no siblings, but had two cousin brothers and they constantly ganged up and teased her. Her friends felt that she was unduly opinionated as far as boys were concerned.

What a stupid looking boy, thought Firan, *and what was he doing spying on us like that -- Nosey Ferozy. What a coincidence that at that very minute I was also peering. Well, I didn't know it was our neighbour's garden on the other side so technically I wasn't spying.* Firan convinced herself. *Boys! Disgusting!*

Her heart was still drumming madly. She wanted to sprawl on the bed or couch and relax, but the whole house was in a mess. There was dust, paper and clothes... all littered, all over the place.

What a mess. Better go back to my room before Mom finds me here, doing nothing. She mumbled.

She went to her room and took out her secret diary and wrote:

Dear Diary,

We have reached. Our new house is good but I don't know about our neighbour. Well, Aunty and Uncle might be ok, but that boy sure is weird. Can you imagine he was trying to spy on us while we were unpacking? Who knows what he might have done if I hadn't been around, he would have entered our garden and maybe looked through the window to see what we were doing. Yes, I think that was his plan. I will have to be alert and keep an eye on him. Boys are like this. They are always creating trouble. I am sure 'Nosey Ferozy' is going to be a pain in the neck.

I hope I won't be in the same school as his. If I am I might have to borrow his copies to complete my work. His copies will surely be untidy and incomplete.

Oh! How irritating! I wonder if he has a sister. I didn't see one when everybody came out.

Please god, please... let me be in a different school. Please.... Please ...Please.

5
Site School Seeing

Firan was a dreamer, always lost in her make believe world. Her world was full of non living things that talked to her, or so she imagined. Gruffy, for instance always said 'Best of luck' to her for all her exams, and she always hugged it before going out anywhere.

In her old house there was a backyard where she and her friends used to play a lot. There was a long rod of iron jutting out of the ground in the shape of a 2. Something like this ⌐ Firan used to spend a lot of time talking to it when she was alone. She had even named it 'Ducky'. If her friends knew that she talked to inanimate objects they would have called her silly, so she had kept it a secret from all her friends.

How she wished she didn't have to go to school at all. Firan dreamed on, *how nice it would be if I was born so intelligent that there was no schooling required.* She sighed, and got back to preparing for her oncoming entrance exams in various schools. Her parents had shortlisted three schools after doing a thorough research on the internet and of course, asking nearly anyone and everyone they met on the road. She sulked when she remembered that one of the three school was the one in which 'Nosey Ferozy' went. How terrible it would be if she had to go to the same school.

Gruffy said 'Best of Luck' and Firan gave it a hug. Today she had an entrance exam in two of the three schools, one of which was Feroz's school, Hyacinth Senior Secondary School. Dad was taking her while Mom was staying back to get the house more organised.

They first went to Feroz's school. She liked the building instantly. It was made with huge boulders and there were many trees all around. They stepped into the corridor and immediately felt an inviting cool breeze. Firan went into the hall where she had to write her exam, there were several children already seated and ready. She felt jittery. The invigilator came in and distributed the question paper and sheets of plain papers for writing the answers.

'I am Miss Rohini and I teach English in this school, please do not feel nervous, just relax and write to the best of your knowledge,' the invigilator said. And then she asked them to start.

Firan looked at all the questions quickly and felt that if she had prepared properly, she could have done well. She looked all around her, nearly all the children were already writing earnestly.

She looked at the invigilator and found that she was looking at her.

'Any problem?' the invigilator asked lifting her eyebrows.

Firan shook her head and looked down at the question paper, and started writing. Halfway through her work she glanced at the invigilator and found that she was looking at her again.

Why is the teacher looking only at me? Wondered Firan, *maybe she thinks I am going to cheat or something.*

She looked out of the window; she could see a classroom full of children on the opposite side. There was a small pathway going up to that classroom. Along the path on one edge was an iron rod shaped exactly like a 2. *Oh! 'Hello, Ducky so you have come here?* Firan said in her mind. There was a clatter of a pencil box falling which brought her back to the question paper.

She hurried on to write down the answers. When she finished the invigilator took the papers and said that the results would be communicated on phone.

Firan and her father then went to the second school in their list, Shamroc International School. Everything was spic and span here. The building had a very posh look. From the foyer Firan could see several doors; some open, some closed. There were three floors full of rooms. In the centre there was a ground / play area and on all the four sides there were corridors and rooms. Some children were playing in the ground and they were actually trying to play without making noise.

How can we play without making noise; I don't want to join this school, Firan thought instantly.

She kept a sullen face when the Principal asked her a few questions. She was then asked to write a page about herself and which subject she liked the best and why. (200 words)

She started writing and after many bad starts she got going. After writing for some time she felt at loss.

How can I write about myself? It is like I am preening…. What more can I write, pondered Firan, *am I helpful?* She glanced again at what she had written.

It did not look nice with so many cuts. *Maybe I should start all over again and write a bit neatly,* and so she started again.

My name is Firan. I am thirteen years old. I love out door games. I have many friends. I am fond of nature. I was in charge of the Environment Club in my old school. We planted many saplings all around our school ground. When I was leaving they had grown about three feet in height. I felt very proud of taking care of them and of their healthy growth. When I grow up I want to be either a veterinary surgeon or a police woman. My mother says I am a 'day dreamer' it may be partially true.

Of all the subjects, I think I like Mathematics because we can use it a lot in our daily lives. Sometimes I like Science. Science is interesting and from science we can know how different things function. I am sure of one thing I don't enjoy Social Science at all. I don't know why we need to study so deeply of events that have already occurred and are over now. I also like English. I like poems by Wordsworth. I like reading stories. My favourite Author is J K Rowling and favourite storybook is Harry Potter and Prisoners of Azkaban.

While she was writing, her father got a call from Hyacinth Senior Secondary School that she had cleared the exam. They could immediately pay the fees and collect the booklist and uniform details from the office. They expected Firan to join as soon as possible as she had already missed many classes.

When Firan came out her father informed her about the offer. He called up home and her parents discussed then and there about the offer. They did not want to waste more time over this and agreed that Firan should join Hyacinth School immediately. Everything started happening fast after that. They rushed back to the school and then to the book store.

Armed with new books, uniform and shoes they reached home.

Firan informed Gruffy that happy days were over. It was going to be Feroz's school after all. Firan hoped and prayed that Feroz wouldn't be in her class.

6
Day One

It was Firan's first day in school. Her father left her outside her classroom. She entered the class and the class teacher introduced her to the class and made her sit in the first row. She tried to steal glances at all the children. There was Feroz!

Why? Why, O God, he had to be in this class and section? She glanced at all the girls. Some of the girls were looking back at her. One of them smiled. Firan smiled back, just a little.

The Class teacher asked Anaida to give her note books to Firan one subject at a time.

Oh! So Anaida is the goody-goody student, the kinds who are always doing the 'correct things' and all the teachers like them.

Firan was never the one in that bracket. A few teachers liked her in the old school but not all. In fact she felt some did not like her at all.

The moment the Teacher left the class room nearly all the girls crowded around Firan.

Girl 1: 'So you are new here huh?'

Firan nodded though she wanted to say 'Hello? Don't you think so?'

Girl 2: 'Where have you come from?'

Firan: 'Mumbai'

Girl 2: 'I have been to Mumbai, Its nice, but it kind of stinks'

Firan: 'Maybe'

Girl 3: 'Those who live there get used to it'

Firan: 'Maybe'

Girl 3: 'Have you seen any of our actors, Shahrukh? Amitabh??'

Firan: 'Nope'

Girl 1: 'Are you sure you are coming from Mumbai?'

All the girls started giggling.

Firan to Girl 1: 'So you must have seen the Prime Minister several times?'

Girl 1: 'no'

Firan: 'Are you sure you are living here in Delhi.

All the girls started giggling again.

Anaida: 'Come on girls, let's not fight. Its Firan's first day and we shouldn't pull her legs today.

See I told you popular Miss Goody Goody Anaida thought Firan to herself

Anaida: 'Let me introduce you to everyone'

She pointed at Girl 1 and said 'that's Romi', then she pointed Girl 2 'that's Joyce', Girl 3 'that's 'Priya.'

The rest of day passed in a blur for Firan, so many things to catch up with, she kept herself aloof feeling very superior, not wanting to mix up with 'these girls and boys' of this school.

Soon the bell rang and everyone rushed to form queues to board their school buses. Firan got pushed around a lot as she didn't exactly know where to go. Someone pushed her so hard that her bag, which she never zipped, fell. Her pencil box, books and all the things rolled out of her bag. She turned to see who had pushed her and found Feroz rushing on ahead totally oblivious of what he had done. She followed him into the bus guessing that probably their buses would also be the same. Feroz stood standing talking to some boy and as soon as the bus started he got off and ran and got into another bus. Firan stood their shocked unable to move or shout for the bus to stop. After quite some time she came to her senses and asked a few kids around whether the bus would go to her locality.

'No, you have got into the wrong bus; you have to take Bus No 13A. Stop... Stop.' Everybody yelled

They made the bus stop. She had to get down and wait for 13A which it seems would be going down the same road a little later. The whole bus waited for her, she felt miserable as she could feel everybody's hostile eyes on her. She knew it was hot and stuffy inside the bus and everyone wanted to be on their way home.

After what seemed like eternity to Firan they saw 13A making its way towards them. It stopped and she got in. The bus in-charge was very angry with her.

'Do you know how much time we wasted looking for you, thankfully while we were looking someone informed me that you had gone in 14A. You should have waited in the 'New Student's queue', now go and sit,' the bus in-charge said in a condescending tone.

Everyone in 13A craned their neck to see who this new girl was, getting up instead of getting down in the middle of their route. Firan saw Feroz wink at one of his friend and she wondered whether it was all planned. She could feel her face go red with anger; she felt exasperated and sorry for herself. Tears welled up in her eyes but she swallowed hard and looked away so that no one could see her face. She resolved she would teach him a lesson.

Soon she saw the bus entering a familiar area. She got off at the bus stop. She noticed that Feroz, three more boys, two of whom were probably in her own section and three girls also get off at the same stop. All of them crossed the road together, then Feroz and she turned towards right and the rest of them went off in the opposite direction.

As soon as she reached her house, Firan rushed to her room and shut the door. Her mother got worried and asked through the closed door whether everything was ok. Firan did not reply the first time, when her Mom asked again she yelled out that it was a horrible school, the children were rude to her and she broke down crying. Her mother knocked on the door a little later and asked her to open the door and share all that happened

'You will feel better,' her Mom implored.

Firan had calmed down by then so she opened the door went straight to the dining room for her lunch. Her mother tried to ask and discuss the events but Firan did not feel like sharing anything. She put on the TV and refused to talk. When her Mom insisted she said. 'I know what you will say Mom... and anyway I am feeling fine now.'

Lately Firan had been going through this phase of defiance and revolt. Mrs Manu Amir thought that it was an adolescent thing and tried to give her a lot of space. Col Amir, though felt differently he had no tolerance and believed that kids should never behave badly. They should always keep their emotions under check.

They had their lunch silently. Firan noticed that her Mom was feeling dejected yet she did not offer to say anything at all. After lunch she retreated back to her room, locked herself and took out her diary and wrote down her pent up frustrations:

Dear Diary,

Horrible first Day at School, horrible, horrible, horrible!! I hate everybody in my school. I hate my new school. Why? Why? God why? is Feroz in my school, same class and same section too? I am never ever .....ever ....going to ask you anything... ever. BYE

7
The Hideout

A Soft breeze entered Firan's room through the window and brushed her hair slightly. It circled the room and blew out as quietly as it had entered.

The weekend had arrived and Firan woke up late. The house was still getting set up. There was an undercurrent of where exactly to place the sofas and which pictures to hang where.

Warning! Warning! War about to begin warned Firan's head. *Better get out of the battlefield,* and she stepped out of the house and went into the garden.

Firan loved to explore new places. So she set off exploring the nook and corners of the area.

She looked at the area where the episode of 'Finding Feroz' had happened. She decided to avoid that direction and headed in the opposite direction. Casuarinas, Banyan, Ashoka, Guava, Banana, Neem and numerous other unknown trees and bushes lined this side. There were a few mango trees too, with lush leaves that were velvety green; they even had some very dark green, small sized mangoes. Two lemon trees swayed just a little and a very pleasant faint lemony smell wafted around. Behind all these trees were all kinds of shrubs, bushes and some more trees. Firan scrambled pushing aside some overgrown bush and then went down on her fours and went further into the foliage. When she emerged on the other side she saw an unbelievable beautiful glade. It was a small clearing with roots of few trees jutting out forming a nice pedestal to sit on.

Yes! She said to herself, *this is the exact spot where I will come and play. This place is so deep inside no one will see me, perfect!*

Firan sat there and she closed her eyes and took a deep breath. She smelt the mud, the leaves, the flowers and some other smells that she wasn't sure about. She turned right and saw some butterflies fleeting up and down and just not settling on any flower, restless it glided away. She looked left; her view was obstructed by the huge trunk of a banyan tree. She turned around and looked behind more bushes and some more trees, how beautiful and secretive everything looked here. She turned around once more, and in front of her were the huge bushes through which she had just come, only if she stood on her toes could she see her house. She looked up, the light blue sky looked down at her, and she was partly under the branches of trees. There was one branch looking like an outstretched hand with knobby and elongated fingers beckoning the sky to come a little closer so that it could grab it.

Firan looked down and gave a start; there was a cat very near her -- looking at her. She froze. Her mouth became dry. She just stood there terrified and looked straight back at the cat unable to move. Motionless! They stood looking at each other for what seemed like hours and suddenly the cat mewed and vanished behind the tree trunk. Firan gathered her wits and told herself *'you idiot it is just a cat!'* She went behind the trunk and all around but couldn't find the cat anywhere in sight.

How mysterious, where has it gone? Wondered Firan, she looked all around again and up the tree, it wasn't there. She stood still and tried to hear a telltale rustling. She didn't hear any rustling, but a mild breeze started blowing exactly where she stood. The breeze brought with itself some far off murmurings; she tried to judge the direction from where she was hearing the voices. The breeze stopped just as suddenly as it had started and so did the murmurings.

She dismissed the occurrences thinking that maybe there was somebody talking beyond the growth or maybe there was a road close by and the voices just carried over. She jumped when she heard her mother shouting.

'Firan...Firan.'

She rushed out and ran home. Her mother saw her coming from behind the trees.

'What were you doing in those bushes, be careful where you play... really...' her mother intoned, ' I have so much work and you just vanish from sight, can't you help a little bit and ....,' on and on she went.

Firan was barely listening. She was in fact thinking about her new secret place.

I wonder where the cat came from and where it vanished, thought Firan later in her room. She had finished her dinner and now was the time to do some extra reading or finish her pending school work.

After she had finished her work, she looked out of the window in the general direction of the secret place. It was well covered and she couldn't see the clearing from the window.

Good! Thought Firan *it is well hidden. How exciting! It is so much more fun exploring places than going to school. I don't know why the nomads settled down in one place. It would have been so nice just going from place to place and exploring the world, most importantly not going to any school.*

Feroz meanwhile was going out with his family to watch the movie 'Pirates of the Caribbean'. They were going for the night show which was beginning at around 9pm, so they decided to have their dinner at some restaurant and then go for the movie. Ajay was also coming along.

'Let's go to a Chinese restaurant,' Feroz suggested.

So 'Ching Ling' it was. They had a sumptuous dinner of Hakka noodles, Sweet and Sour, Veg Manchurian, Spring Rolls, Ginger Garlic rice in Bamboo shoot. Then they went to an ice-cream parlour. Feroz looked at the variety of ice creams and chose 'Minty chocolate'; Ajay had 'Nutty chocolate'. Feroz felt very happy and eagerly looked forward to the movie.

The movie was excellent - a perfect way to end a wonderful evening. On the way back from the movie, Feroz noticed that it was an unusually dark night; the car was zipping silently and smoothly. The traffic was thin and his dad was travelling at good speed. Ajay and Feroz started dozing behind.

'Oh there are no street-lights today,' said Mrs Shah, 'hope there is no load shedding tonight.'

Feroz opened his eyes and stuck his head in between the front seats and looked straight outside, *Yes, it did seem quite dark.*

As they neared their locality he noticed some dogs on the road. He perked up when he saw that there were quite a few; almost twenty; even his Mom and dad were looking keenly. The strangest part was that all of them looked similar. There was no mistaking that they were street dogs.

'Uff... so many dogs,' said Mrs Shah.

Dr. Shah slowed a bit, Feroz could now see that all the dogs had straw coloured coats with a conspicuous big black patch, it seemed as if they were having a meeting of sorts. The leader of the pack stood tall and bold and glared at their car. Feroz felt his skin tingle as if electric charges were colliding with each other right on his skin. It seemed as if the dog was about to chase the car, but it didn't. The car passed and Feroz turned back and took one last look at this magnificent dog. The rest of the dogs were all huddling around this leader. *A congregation of street dogs, planning the future of planet Earth*, thought Feroz.

Feroz froze... *cat, snake, dogs, mynahs, all the birds and animals in this vicinity were behaving strangely.*

8
Cat...merising

Feroz always knew when he was dreaming. His dreams always began with him being very, very small in size, almost ant size and he would be in a huge, huge room that was fully tiled, white tiles. He would be in a corner looking up and the roof would be far, far up. After this scene his dream would change to something new. Tonight he was running, encountering strange obstacles, jumping over rocks and boulder, climbing half constructed building which had iron rods sticking out. He couldn't make out why he was running, who was behind him. He didn't dare look back but he knew by intuition that whoever was following him was closing the gap, and was almost upon him. He takes a leap from the top of what looked like the wall of an unconstructed building to reach another half constructed building on the opposite side and right there his dream stopped.

He moved just a little, half opened his eyes and looked at the clock, it was 3 a.m. He groaned, *why did*

I wake up? He dropped his head on the pillow and tried to reconstruct his dream making purposeful attempts to end it favourably, as if he landed safely on the other side. Somehow it did not seem right and he gave up.

'Feroz, Feroz get up beta its 6 o'clock, you will miss your school bus...,'said his Mom.

Feroz groaned, he was feeling so tired, it was as if he had done a lot of work, all his bones were aching.

'Mom, let me sleep for five more minutes, pleeeeeze,' he pleaded and snuggled deeper into the pillow.

His Mom pottered around in the room setting his books and clothes in order. She stopped to read some gibberish that was scribbled on a piece of paper trying to decipher what was written. She couldn't make out what was written, she thought of throwing it in the dustbin then on second thought decided to leave it there on the table. Feroz somehow got ready and reached the bus stop on time.

The bell rang and it was science period. Firan loved science classes, especially biology. She loved all living things and wanted to know everything about them. While waiting for the science class to begin she started thinking, *perhaps I should become a biologist, though I don't know what a biologist would be doing at work. May be I should stick to becoming a Vet?*

Batra Sir entered the class room and immediately she heard the word 'moody' being whispered back and forth between students. Sir came in and took up his position behind the teacher's desk.

'I have brought another pet of mine,' said Batra Sir.

From a basket he took out a....Cat!

Firan shrieked and everybody jumped, a few chairs crashed on the floor.

'Calm down, calm down....Yes? you new student! What is your problem? Are you scared? Haven't you seen a cat before, they are harmless poor creature. What a ruckus you have created,' Sir shouted.

He turned and found that in the confusion the cat was not there on the table. He bent down looking under the table and turned left and right. It just wasn't there. All the children watched quietly, now Sir would lose his temper and his mood will change, all because of that new girl. They all glared at Firan. Firan avoided their eyes and looked down and gave out an even louder shriek. The cat was right there at her feet, looking at her. Everybody jumped again, Sir rushed towards her and lifted the cat and put it back into the basket and asked Firan to get out of the room. She ran out tears flowing down her cheeks.

She went into the girls washroom and cried some more. She waited for quite some time constantly wiping her tears. She heard the bell go. She dreaded going back to the class. What a fool she had made of herself.

She waited outside the classroom for quite sometime, and when she saw her Maths teacher enter the classroom. She quickly went in, right behind her. She could feel everybody staring at her. She busied herself with her face practically inside her bag, looking for her Maths book and copy. The Teacher started teaching straight away. She gave them all some sums and started checking by walking along the aisle to see if everybody was doing them correctly.

Priya mumbled, 'Ma'am does all the easy ones while explaining and we have to do difficult ones ourselves. This is not fair!'

Firan was doing them quite easily and when Ma'am passed her table she said a loud 'good', that cheered her and she worked hard and completed all the sums, and got them all correct too. Priya was struggling with them; Firan helped her a little, pointing out her mistakes as she was doing them. Thus the Maths class passed easily.

The rest of the day things went on smoothly, except during the last period. They had music in the last period and were in the music room. They were writing down the wordings of a song when suddenly at the entrance the cat made a sudden appearance. Firan noticed it only after everyone had started pointing it out, so she was more composed.

The cat made a majestic entry; it looked, turned and started strolling towards Firan. Everybody moved aside, the cat seemed to know where it wanted to go! Firan remained calm and kept looking at it. It kept walking and came straight to where she was standing and looked up at her, everybody watched totally mesmerized, nobody spoke. Firan was feeling very scared, but she did not want to create a scene, she kept telling herself 'it is only a cat, it is only a cat... it is only a cat, it is only a cat. Now the cat was near her feet, Firan hoped that it would not jump on her. The cat turned around now facing the rest of the class and just stood beside her. All the students were standing absolutely still, there was pin drop silence. Even the music teacher was standing still, as if somebody had said 'Statue'.

The science teacher suddenly appeared at the door way and started to say

'Did you......' and he stopped short.

'What's going on?' He said taking in the scene.

Everybody started moving and speaking simultaneously. Firan took a step back; The Science Sir looked at her and the cat at her feet. He strode forward picked up the cat and glared at Firan and left. Firan looked down and felt bad.

Why did Sir glare at me? She wondered.

All her classmates saw it and went to sympathise with her. 'Why did Moody glare at poor Firan?' They murmured.

'That too when she was being so brave,' said Joyce.

The bell rang; everybody jumped at the sudden noise and scrambled to collect their belongings, talking at the same time. All of them said 'bye' to each other and especially to Firan. She was accepted into their fold. They would include her as their friends for sure. All of them chattered all the way to the school buses, many of her new friends who were travelling in her bus continued to talk animatedly. Feroz was also hanging around with them, though he didn't say much.

That night Firan replayed the whole episode in her mind. She kept seeing the two large eyes of the cat focused on her. She speculated... was it the same one that she had seen in the hideout? Why did it keep looking at her? Was it seeking her?

9
Trri...ng Tri...ng Buzz...

'Let's make a club,' said Bonty when they met for Sunday morning cricket and they started to make all sorts of plans for it.

'We can call it Fab Club,' said Feroz.

'F for Feroz, A for Ajay and B for Bonty,' explained Feroz.

'No,' said Ajay, 'let's have it in alphabetical order, ABF club.'

'Hey, it was my idea,' said Bonty, 'let's name it Baf Club.'

'It need not mean anything,' he added.

Nobody wanted to give in so they decided to let the matter be for some time and think of a proper name later on.

Later in the afternoon Feroz was in his room supposed to be doing his homework, but he kept thinking of different names for their club. He opened his math book and started working on fractions. Midway through, he stopped and said aloud 'The fraction Club?' *No, they might have to solve problems in fraction to keep that name.* He moved on to his science work and started turning pages to see if he could find some interesting word that could be used for the name of their club. *The Atom Club, or maybe... Hydrogen?*

His Mom suddenly entered the room

'What are you doing?' she asked Feroz.

His Mom had this uncanny habit of knowing when he was doing something other than what he was supposed to be doing. He pretended to get back to work and did not reply. He picked up his English Literature and started flipping the pages. *Tom Sawyer Club? The three musketeers? No. It has to be original. Simile, Metaphor, 'how about 'Metafour' Club?' but then we are only three,* thought Feroz.

He looked out of his window. *Hey, that cat again.* He rushed to his window. The cat mewed. He peered out to see if the secret of the cat would be revealed today, if he just watched carefully and patiently. At first he couldn't see where it was hiding, he could only hear it and suddenly it appeared from nowhere. It looked here and there for sometime, he saw it jump across towards a broken pot, lying upside down. It seemed to be crouching under it.

Oh! That's where it lives.

Trri...ng Tri...ng buzz... the telephone ring broke the silence of the house, Feroz jumped and rushed to answer the call before anybody else could get it. He snatched it from the cradle and said

'Hello...Hello?'

No reply. He stopped breathing and tried to listen, pressing the telephone hard on his ears. Still he could hear nothing. He put the phone down and thought may be his friends were playing a prank on him. Or it could be a kidnapper checking whether he was alone in the house. He waited for sometime willing the phone to ring again. It did not.

He picked the phone and dialled a random number 7 7 2 3 4 1 2 2. He could hear the ring going but nobody picked up on the other side. He felt disappointed. He tried again, 7 2 7 3 5 3 5 3 another random number, almost immediately he heard a voice

'Hello?'

It was a man voice.

'Hello, can I speak to Tom?' said Feroz

'Tom? There is nobody by that name here and I don't think there is anybody by the name Tom that you want to talk to. I think you have purposely dialled some vague number and are pretending to act like you want to speak to Tom.'

Feroz was stunned, his tongue felt very heavy and refused to move, his mind went absolutely blank. 'Hello?' the voice said again 'dumb struck huh?'

'Feroz, Feroz put the phone down,' bellowed his Mom.

Feroz put the phone down hurriedly hoping that the man had not heard his Mom shouting his name.

The cat started to mew ever so loudly now. Feroz snapped his books shut and made up his mind to check out the cat first and then go to Ajay's house for playing.

He ran out of the house and headed to the garden, he tilted the pot just a little and crouched down and peered, there was nothing underneath it. It must have run away, he put the pot down, and down jumped the cat from a nearby tree. It started dashing away.

Feroz decided to follow it. It dashed and stopped and then started strolling again, Feroz followed it quite a long distance, in fact he even crossed Ajay's house. He realized that the cat was going towards their school bus stop, the route which Ajay and others used. He slowed down when saw that the cat was heading towards the shack where that crazy-dog-man lived. He heard some shuffling behind him and he turned, lo and behold the crazy man was standing just behind him also looking at the cat entering the shack.

'Yes?' the man asked.

'Umm....,' said Feroz.

'Yes, what do you want?'

Feroz racked his brain to say something meaningful and intelligent, but he just kept looking -- blankly. The man said 'Dumb struck huh?'

Feroz panicked when he heard those words for the second time today. He took to heels, not stopping for even a second till he reached Ajay's house.

Ajay and Bonty were already playing in the ground near Ajay's house. They had completely lost interest in the crazy-dog-man and had not brought up the topic of visiting the shack at all. According to them may be Yapra knew the pattern in which that dog barked, maybe it always barked in that order.

Both of them never paid any attention to nature. They were only interested in playing games. Feroz was unlike them in this regards, he revelled in the mystery of nature and surroundings. He loved observing anything from ants to humans. For him life held secrets and you need to discover them.

Now he contemplated *How?... was it possible? Was the man who talked with him on the phone none other than the crazy-dog-man? Why were these episodes happening to him?*

Seeing Feroz just standing there, Bonty yelled.

'Wake up sleepy head, what are you thinking about?'

Feroz narrated the incident. It was clear that he was really shaken and upset. Ajay, the most sensible of the three, said 'Look, this man saying 'dumb stuck' might be pure coincidence.'

Bonty impatient as ever said, 'Just forget about all this yaar and let's just... you keep yourself occupied... don't think about all this weird stuff. Ignore them... they won't haunt you then'

Ajay agreed with Bonty and added 'You get Yapra especially out of your mind. It is no good thinking about him all the time. He is just a vagabond.'

10
Partner Found

The next day in the evening Firan's Mom asked her to go and explore the colony and see if she could make some new friends. Reluctantly, Firan headed out, she wanted to go to her hideout, but she didn't want to argue with her mother. Also if she insisted that she would spend time in the garden her mother would become suspicious and maybe try and follow her, she did not want that.

The best time of the day according to Feroz was five in the evening, he loved it because it was the only time he felt truly free. Nothing nagged his brains at this time of the day.

He resolved that he would forget all the recent stupid incidences and go for cycling. His Mom looked very happy when he said he was going to cycle. She always went on and on about physical activity. 'When we were kids....' his parents would start narrating, 'we did this, that... etc' and privately Feroz always wanted to avoid listening about it.

His mother warned him to ride carefully before she went off for her own walk. Feroz wondered why his mother went for walks -- it seemed so boring.

He decided he would check what Ajay and Bonty were up to and persuade them for a bicycle race. Today he felt sure he would win the race. He cycled slowly feeling the strain in his calf muscles, -- a wonderful ache. Ajay wasn't there at home, but Bonty joined him.

Along the road in a particular area there was a huge mound of mud, a sort of a land mark for the residents of Park Lane, Dhaula Kuan. According to Feroz 'it has been there since time immemorial.' It changed its shape and size depending on the weather. In summer, its feature resembled a dry, parched dead land and during rainy season it looked disgusting, with water and mud forming a big slush on the road so that everybody avoided going through that lane. In winters, it looked quite harmless; people actually brought out their mats and sat on the sunny side of it, moving their mats as the direction of the sunlight changed.

The kids of the colony loved this mound during summers. They would challenge each other to cycle up and down in full speed and not fall. Feroz's Mom had strictly prohibited him from cycling up the mound. He watched as Bonty showed off his skill, going up and down the mound attracting a lot of attention.

He felt very excited looking at Bonty and all the attention he was getting from everybody, especially the girls and more especially from Tia. Squashing the small voice that was telling him not to cycle up that mound, he rushed at full speed and stopped at the top, posed nicely and let himself go. That small voice in his head sighed and almost immediately he hit a stone, and lost his hold on the bike. He flew leftwards and hit the ground and rolled uncontrollably downhill, his bike followed a different course and tumbled this way and that and finally settled at the bottom of the mound right before Tia and gang.

Feroz watched as if in slow motion, everybody surrounded him. Bonty helped him up, someone brought his cycle. He felt embarrassed, hot tears swelled in his eyes. He felt as if he had shrunk to the size of an ant. Suddenly he felt angry and brushed away the helping hands of Bonty and others. He shouted 'I'm ok.'

Everybody backed off. Feroz got on his bike and cycled away. He felt humiliated.

He cycled around the corner and slowly went into bi-lanes and turned several corners. Then he got off and examined his bike for scratches and dents. There were many. His tracks were also torn at the knee, there was a rough cut above his knee and spots of blood were blotting on it. *How could such a nice evening turn so horrible? Was it because he had not listened to his Mom?* That voice in his head had distracted him, he hated it. 'I will never allow it to say anything ever' he promised himself.

He continued to ride his bike which was now making a clang - clang noise. Every time the pedal came up it went 'clang'. He returned to the main road which ran all around the colony. As he cycled he saw Firan walking along the road.

He cycled slowly unsure whether to cross her or be just behind her or turn around and go in different direction. His cycle solved his dilemma for it made a loud clang and Firan turned around and looked at him. They spontaneously said

'Hi!'

Feroz did not stop and cycled ahead. He saw the shack up ahead and felt tempted to peek again. He decided at the spur of the moment that he would try and have a meaningful conversation with the crazy-dog-man.

Firan observed that Feroz was going towards a vague hut. She perked up and felt drawn to follow him; she tried to think of why she would want to do that? But, she couldn't come up with an answer. She maintained some distance and kept him in sight. When she saw him disappear inside the shack she hurried on.

When Feroz entered he saw that the man was there, apparently waiting for somebody to enter through the door. As soon as he saw him at the door he stood up and said, 'come, come... don't be afraid.'

Feroz entered and the man extended his hand, 'I'm Yapra; you saw that etched on the wall, didn't you?'

Feroz nodded and asked, 'Did you see us?'

'No,' and he added, 'Ahh, your partner has also arrived.'

Feroz looked surprised when he saw Firan entering through the broken door.

'She is not my partner,' he said quickly.

'We will see about that.' Looking at Firan he said, 'I'm Yapra, come, come sit.'

Firan studied Yapra carefully. He looked her father's age. He was wafer thin; all his joints looked pointed because of his thinness. He had a long face and shoulder length hair tied up in a pony. He had his T-shirt tucked in and a strip of cloth did the job of a belt. Anyone looking at him would have taken a second look; he was such an odd looking man. Yapra was looking at her; there was something about his eyes that was different. The white's of the eyes were absolutely clear and white. His eyes had been intense few seconds back now they twinkled.

A smile formed on his lips and he said, 'Did I pass the examination?'

Firan felt flustered.

'Do you read minds, Mr. Yapra?' she stammered out.

'You are almost right and just call me Yapra'

'Is that how you knew I had read the etching on wall?' asked Feroz.

'No, no..,' he laughed and said, 'remember you cleaned the writing to see what was written? I just guessed that it must have been you.'

'Now I am going to say something that you are not going to accept.' He paused and looked into both their eyes.

Both the children wrinkled their eyebrows.

'It is me who has beckoned you both here, right at this moment. I have chosen you both to share something with you. But, before I tell you, I want you to promise that you will not tell anybody about it.'

Both of them looked flabbergasted at him. Yapra looked at them and felt that these kids would be perfect for the job he needed done.

11
Mind-Blowing

Both of them felt keyed up; everything about this man was mysterious. Yapra waited patiently for their reply. Feroz was the first one to say, 'I promise.' He had vested interest, he wanted to know how Yapra made the dogs bark the way they did.

Firan also uttered the words; she was always game for some thrill and excitement.

Yapra knew he had chosen the right guinea pigs. Both of them were very sensitive to their surroundings. They were aware of things that children of their age group tended to ignore. He just needed them to give him 'a consent' to be a part of his experiment. Once he had their body and mind in his control he could make them do anything.

He looked at their eager faces and decided that he wouldn't need to confide completely. He would share only part of his information and they would surely agree to serve him.

'I am doing an experiment and I need your help. Will you help me? You will enjoy it, I am sure you must be studying about my experiments in your science lessons it will be live examples for you.'

He said all this with a very straight face. He looked completely harmless. What he had said was far from truth. It was not exactly a science experiment and definitely not what the children were studying at this stage. He looked at both of them and asked beseechingly

'Help me please.'

'What do we have to do?' asked Firan

'Nothing right now actually, maybe later, but I need you to give me a consent now.'

'I will help you.' Feroz said quickly. He did not want Firan involved in this.

'And you?' enquired Yapra looking at Firan.

'I can't stay out late and all and... umm... I would need to ask my dad.'

'But I told you, you can't tell anybody about this, you promised.' Yapra said looking alarmed.

'Oh...ok, I will help' she said reluctantly.

'I'm a natural parapsychologist. Do you know what that means?

Both of them shook their heads

'As child I had this capacity to know what someone was thinking and as I grew up I realized that I could read minds. Then I started gathering evidences that such a thing exists. The power of mind is immense. So I started experimenting more and tried to do stuffs like moving an object with the power of my mind, hypnotism, telepathy etc.'

Firan interrupted and asked, 'Did you take a course in this subject?'

'No, that is why I said I'm natural parapsychologist. I learnt everything myself. Right now I am training animals and birds to read my mind and do as I tell them. Feroz you saw what I did last time, didn't you?'

Firan looked at Feroz and thought, *He has been here before! What a curious boy.*

Feroz nodded and said, 'In fact I wanted to ask, did you know I was watching you?'

'The correct question would be did you make me watch it?

Feroz wrinkled his forehead making his eyebrows almost meet... looking completely confused.

'You mean...' he began and stopped.

'Yes, I made you follow me and I did the trick for your benefit.'

Many questions and doubts erupted in Feroz's mind but he did not want to ask them in front of Firan. He wondered whether what he had seen and experienced the other day when he had found his mother missing were maybe Yapra's doings.

Reading his mind accurately Yapra smiled. Undoubtedly he had made it all happen. He wanted Feroz to witness his powers. It wasn't difficult for him to do that because Feroz had on his own started the game of following the shadow of telephone lines and so with his mind already tuned to shadows Yapra just added the mynah's and shadow figures. All that Feroz had seen had really happened under Yapra's directions but Feroz's mind refused to accept it later. It kept suggesting that perhaps Feroz slept off and he started to believe that. Yapra was disappointed and came to realize that though Feroz's mind was susceptible to fantasies it needed more training which could be done only if the individual gave consent to be trained.

Over the years Yapra had perfected the science of reading minds of living things. He had complete control of all the stray dogs of Dhaula Kuan. He could make them charge at someone or follow someone. When the dogs returned he would read their mind and get information about the happenings in the area.

The night when Feroz's car had passed the pack of dogs Yapra had been sitting nearby reading the minds of the stray dogs. The dogs were at that very minute informing him about a mysterious cat that appeared and disappeared at will. Yapra somehow managed to find the cat and made it come to his shack and what he read from its mind was astounding. *There was a world known to its master that was secretive and filled with mystery.* The cat got this information from his master's other pet Specter. His master had taken Specter to this world for a week. Yapra gleaned the general location of this world but couldn't find out how to enter it or what exactly would be there.

Yapra was excited to know more about this world. He realized that he needed somebody to visit this world under a trance and report the details to him.

So he started looking for an ideal person, the person needed to be observant, sensitive and trainable. He chanced upon Feroz after observing him for sometime he decided that he would be the best. He analyzed Feroz's mind when he had peeked into his shack and discovered that it would work to full potential only with an equivalent and encouraging partner.

Luckily the problem was resolved on its own. The universe had the habit of solving Yapra's problems. Firan shifted into their colony, careful observation led Yapra to believe that Firan would be a perfect partner for Feroz. They were similar in many ways as far as sensitivity and vivid imagination was concerned.

He thought that they would become friends instantly but that did not happen. There were still parts that Yapra couldn't understand about working of the minds and this was one of them.

Yapra started becoming more and more impatient because Feroz and Firan refused to gel. In fact they were avoiding each other and their friendship did not bloom naturally. Today was perhaps the first time they had met without squirming away from each other.

Yapra felt elated he would use these two kids to find out about the secret world. He would train their minds now that they had given their consent and make them visit the other world. He himself didn't want to go there because he felt that his life would be in danger.

'Remember I said we will meet again when your partner comes? Here we are... she is your partner; it's interesting the way your minds work, I can safely say that you both have similar minds. They are twin minds.' Yapra said after a long period of silence.

He started laughing after that statement and he laughed like a mad man.

The children felt scared and terrified. Hoping that no harm had been done they ran out of the shack. Firan sprinted away. Feroz grabbed his bike and peddled hard. He reached his house puffing and panting - but safe.

12
Fallen Ladder

Feroz was thinking about Yapra the whole evening. He could hardly concentrate on his home work. He somehow got it done with. He looked out of the window and replayed the conversation with Yapra. He felt a draft through the window. It was a dark night and he could indistinctly make out the garden and Firan's house beyond. He noticed that the light was on in her room. The house was so positioned that he could not see inside her room, but could see if someone stood at the window.

Firan did not want to remember the Yapra episode and she felt that it was a mistake to have agreed to anything the mad man had suggested. She got up to move towards the window and think.

Feroz could make out some movement in Firan's window; he decided to move away from his window lest she peers out of hers and finds him looking.

Just as he moved away from his window, Firan peered from her window. She looked at her hideout and felt excited, if only she could go there now just for a few minutes. She leaned out of the window and looked down. She saw a ladder lying on the ground. She smiled, a naughty plan began forming in her mind, perhaps she could make the ladder lean against her window and maybe visit the 'Hideout' whenever she felt like. She felt totally thrilled at the thought of being in the 'Hideout' at night time.

Feroz parted the curtain to check if she was still looking out, He saw her moving away from the window after looking at something on the ground and smiling.

What was the smile for? He craned his neck to see what she might have looked at and couldn't see anything. *Girls! Are so silly,* he craned some more and then he saw a ladder lying on the grass. *Oooooh! Is she planning to climb down her window using the ladder? She is surely up to something.* Feroz decided that he would be on the lookout for her doing something naughty or mysterious.

The next day Firan set the ladder against her window. Now she only had to wait for a chance. She practiced opening and closing the grill window and the glass window in her room as quietly as possible. 'Sure tis an art' she mused aloud.

Feroz noticed the ladder immediately and he punched in the air, and said, 'I knew it.' *What will she do now? Sneak of somewhere, to her friend's house, maybe. The ladder looked a bit wobbly. Will she be able to climb down without falling?*

The very following day a fantastic opportunity to sneak out arrived for Firan. Her parents had to go out to attend a wedding ceremony. They got ready and instructed her to eat and go to sleep at the right time. They had two doors, one with an auto lock and another grill door which could be bolted from outside. They did that and put a lock on the outside door as well for safety. Whenever they knew that they were going to come back late they followed this procedure for two reasons: one, so that if anyone came to their house they would see the lock and go away; two, Firan need not stay awake to open the door.

It was 7pm, Firan finished the few sums left of her Maths homework and decided to go to 'The Hideout' immediately. She took out a box and filled it up with her dinner and then she put that, a bottle of water and her diary inside a bag. She slung it across her shoulder and after thinking for a second she took a jacket and stuffed it too inside her bag.

All set, she opened the window, first the glass window, then the wire mesh one. It opened effortlessly without squeaking even once. She peered out, yes, the ladder was there. She climbed the window sill and sat on it, *now how to step on the ladder without making it fall?* She extended one of her leg and tried to reach the ladder, she could barely manage to touch it. She felt flummoxed. *How on earth do I get down?* She wondered.

She realized she would need to turn around and then get down. While still sitting on the window sill she turned slowly and then by hanging on her hands she felt for the ladder with her legs. 'I hope I don't kick it,' she murmured. She felt the ladder under her foot, it wobbled dangerously. She placed one foot on the top rung and slowly extended her other foot down the second rung. She placed it firmly on it and let go of one of her hand from the window sill.

'This is not easy,' she said to herself.

She pressed her hand on the wall and felt for a lower rung, she now needed to let go of the other hand which was still holding the window sill. Slowly she slipped her hand down and the ladder wobbled again, her breathing doubled and her heart raced. A thought crossed her mind *What if I fall and break my legs....oh, this is a bad idea.* She waited half hanging, half standing, totally petrified. 'I can't climb back; I can only go down... there is no other way.' She said to herself. She pressed herself against the wall and moved her other foot down another rung. The ladder wobbled again. She quickly brought the other foot also on the same rung, and then she bent a little awkwardly and was now able to hold the top of the ladder. She quickly stepped down one more rung and stood there for some time. Then she slowly climbed down the ladder till she reached the hard ground. She let out a sigh of relief.

She looked up and realized that she had not closed the window. She cursed herself. She didn't want to climb up again, close it and come down. So she brought the ladder down and dragged it a little away from the window. She grunted and thought, *God, this is becoming so much of hard work.* She looked at her watch; all this had taken her nearly 30 minutes. She shrugged her bag tightly and started walking towards the hideout. The moon was out and there was enough light, still she felt she should have brought a torch along.

She didn't feel scared. She crawled under the bushes and shrubs and made her way to the spot where she planned to have her dinner. She felt really hungry now. Once she reached the glade she first surveyed all around to see if it was really safe. 'Now that we have come so far, lets get this over with' she said to herself. She climbed up a thick root and sat down on it. *Hmm... I should have got a mat to sit on.* She then took out her dinner and started eating. She could hear some mild rustling of leaves and a few crickets. Slowly it began to sink in that here she was, doing what she had planned. Her fear vanished and in its place was excitement.

She took out her diary to write down this feeling and all that she had to go through to reach here.

Feroz glanced out of his window while chatting with Bonty on the cordless phone. As was his habit these days he looked straight at Firan's window. *What! Where is the ladder?* He also noticed that Firan's windows were open.

'Oh!' He said on the phone.

'What happened?' asked Bonty

'Nothing, listen I will call back, I need to go, bye ok?' said Feroz and put the cordless down.

Oh! No, how did I miss that? Maybe Firan started getting down and the ladder fell. I should just hide and keep observing. He glanced towards Firan's window it seemed too quiet. *I think she has left that room and is definitely roaming the country side.*

13
Teamed

Feroz decided to go down to his garden and see if he could spot Firan. He went down and was just about to sneak out of the side door when his Mom spotted him.

'Where are you going?' She asked.

'Umm nowhere,' replied Feroz and went back to his room.

He closed his room door and decided to spy through the window itself, he would stay up all night if he needed to. He looked out and who should be climbing up the ladder, none other than Firan. He hid a little and cursed himself again. He had missed the chance of seeing her coming back. She looked very funny climbing the ladder ever so slowly as if she was going to fall the very next minute. *How will she get on the window? This should be fun to watch,* Feroz chuckled.

Firan had four more rungs left to climb; she stretched out her hands to see if she could reach the window, she was short by just a few inches. She went up one more step, now her hands just grazed the sill. She needed to climb up one more step. Now this was the difficult part. Slowly she raised one foot and kept it on the second rung from the top and lifted herself just a little, the ladder shook. Feroz caught his breath; *oops~! The ladder is going to fall!* He saw Firan take a leap and the ladder fall with a thud. Firan was now hanging on the window sill. She then scrambled and with the help of her knees, she crawled up the wall and put one of her legs over the sill and the other one soon followed and she landed with another thud in her room.

Shucks! Surely her knees would be totally scraped and bloody, thought Feroz and got away from the window.

His Mom popped her head in his room and asked 'Did you hear something?

Feroz didn't want to lie so he just moved his eyeballs about indicating neither yes nor no. His Mom shrugged and said 'you go to sleep, have you done your home work?' Feroz nodded and his Mom went away.

Immediately Feroz looked out, the lights were off in Firan's room and the windows were now, closed. He put his own room light off. A few minutes later he heard the sound of Firan's dad's car coming and the closing of the gates. So that's why Firan went out today! He was curious to know where she had gone but there was no way to know that.

The next day at the bus stop Feroz couldn't keep his eyes off Firan. He glanced at the injury on her knees, it looked terrible. One knee had a deep cut, *surely that must be hurting*. Firan though looked upbeat and happy, definitely not in pain. She was chatting with a boy in X Std. Bonty and Ajay were chattering intermittently and making action of batting and bowling an imaginary ball.

Yapra was observing both of them from far. He was secretly keeping a watch on both of them. He was creating situations so that both these kids would be forced to become friends. It was clear that it was not happening naturally he had to intervene. 'So be it,' he said to himself 'I will make it happen.'

Feroz was so curious to know where Firan had gone that the whole time in school he just couldn't concentrate on anything else. He was constantly trying to listen to whatever she was saying to her friends in the hope of finding out where she had sneaked off. He had no luck in knowing that because Firan had no intentions of sharing her secret with anybody.

After the lunch break, the whole class was talking non stop and creating so much of a racket that nobody noticed the Class Teacher, Mrs Anita enter. She stood there for sometime fuming and at the same time trying to be patient. When the noise didn't subdue, she shouted at the top of her voice 'Stand up all of you'.

As if brought to their senses everybody stopped talking and stood up. There was a deafening silence.

'THIS CLASS IS FILLED WITH STUDENTS WHO HAVE NO MANNERS.' She shouted, 'You are so busy chatting that you didn't even see that your teacher has entered. Who are the class monitors?'

Priya and Rahul stood up.

'So the class monitors are also sitting and creating ruckus,' she carried on; 'Joyce surely I am not telling a joke, why are you smiling?' fumed Mrs Anita.

Joyce immediately put her head down.

'All of you take your bags and stand out side the class room that ought to quieten you down and ensure that your desks are empty and all your belongings are in your bag. Hurry up' she ordered.

Everybody picked up their bags and hurriedly stuffed them with the things from inside the desk. They stood outside in a row.

'As long as we are in it together,' whispered Joyce into Firan's ears.

After 15 minutes Mrs Anita called the monitors inside and asked them to set the table and chairs in neat rows. As soon as they had finished doing that she said

'I want all the students to form a line - 'height wise'.

The monitors fervently got down to the task, they didn't want to annoy Anita ma'am further. They first asked the boys to make a queue so that the shortest child, Anuj, was in front and the rest of them stood behind Anuj in ascending order of height. A similar queue was made for the girls also.

Ajay, Bonty and Feroz were nearly of the same height and stood one behind the other.

Everyone was wondering whether they were going to be marched up to the Principal. But that was not what the class teacher had in mind.

She called the students one by one and allotted them their seats. She ensured that friends were not sitting together. The quieter ones were sitting with the talkative ones and the naughty ones were sitting with the serious ones and so on.

Ajay, Bonty and Feroz found themselves in entirely different rows. Feroz found himself seated next to Firan!

'Monitors, you have to ensure that no one and I emphasize, no one is allowed to change their seat in any of the periods. Am I clear?'

Everybody nodded.

'Now, take out your books, we have already wasted much time,' ordered the class teacher.

Rest of the day passed quite seriously for all of them. They felt rather unhappy.

Feroz on the other hand was not that unhappy. *Here is a chance to befriend Firan and find out where she headed* thought Feroz.

Yapra's intentions were beginning to take shape. Now that he had their consent he could manipulate the events that had to do with them. He had to ensure that they became friends. Unknown to them he had already started the experiment. They thought that they were going about their normal routine and that all that had happened in the shack was meaningless. Yapra had their thought process tweaked like that. The experiment was already underway, in two days it would take momentum.

14
Teamed Again

Feroz didn't attempt to talk to Firan, for one thing he didn't know how to start and another she looked away 100% of the time. She was behaving as if nobody was sitting next to her.

What is her problem? Wondered Feroz

The day passed and Feroz could not glean anything from the conversation that he managed to eavesdrop. At the end of the day they got into their buses. Feroz and his friends sat together and had an animated discussion of all the events that happened. Ajay was sitting with Manoj. Bonty was sitting with Anaida. Both were ok with their partners. They asked Feroz how his partner was. Feroz just shrugged his shoulders and changed the conversation. He was beginning to dislike the word 'partner'.

'Let's meet at the cricket ground in the evening,' said Feroz to change the subject and they agreed.

They got off their bus and as usual Feroz and Firan turned in one direction and the rest of the crowd went off in the other direction. Feroz contemplated kicking a stone but gave up. He saw Firan hurrying ahead. *Where could she have gone? I wonder whether she will try again tonight.*

He saw her stop in front her gate and look at something. As he walked up he saw that she was staring at a huge lock which was hanging on the gate. He also stopped.

'Umm, would you like to come to my house and wait for your Mom to get back?'

'No I am ok' replied Firan.

'Umm, it is not a problem, what will you do otherwise?'

'Don't worry I will climb over the gate and wait in the garden'.

She hung her bag over the top of the gate and climbed up and over the gate, and jumped down on the other side. She brought her bag down and looked at Feroz through the gate.

'Bye,' she said and turned away.

Feroz stood there for a minute, murmured 'bye' to himself and started going towards his own house.

He was in bad mood when he reached his house. He had his gulp of water from the fridge and rushed to his room. *Maybe Firan will head out again.* He rushed to the window to take a peak. His Mom had kept a pot of house plant on the sill for some exposure to the sun. He leaned over it and instantly knocked the pot. He shouted

'Oh!

At that exact moment Firan looked up and saw him looking at her. Their eyes met and remained locked for a little while before Firan quickly looked away. Feroz looked down at the pot which was gathering momentum and hurtling down. He saw with alarm that their visiting pet, the cat was curled up right below. He started yelling and clapping to make the cat move out. The cat didn't budge and the pot plummeted down and crashed right on it. There was resounding thud of the crashing pot. Hearing the thud his Mom yelled from somewhere inside the house.

'What happened?'

Firan heard the thud and looked up realizing that something had happened.

Feroz just stood rooted there, his eyes nearly popped out when he saw the cat get up stretch and amble away from the debris.

The incident of the cat sobered down Feroz's curiosity about Firan's jaunt and reverted to the mysterious cat.

The rest of the evening he did not spy on Firan. He stayed in his room called Ajay and told him he won't be coming for cricket. Ajay told him that even he was not going as his Mom was upset with his 7/10 marks in Maths class test. He went on and on about it and how unfair everything was. He kept saying 'it is only a class test, what's the big deal?'

Feroz empathized with Ajay. He had got an 8/10 and Bonty had a 10/10.

Next day Firan went up to Feroz at the bus top and asked point blank 'What happened yesterday?'

He was surprised that she had come to talk to him, he wasn't prepared. He stuttered 'Umm...what?'

'What was the commotion all about yesterday, after we got back from school? She asked.

'Oh that!' explained Feroz 'a pot fell from my window sill and...umm...it landed straight on a cat which lives in our garden,' he paused and blurted, 'It survived!'

'Oh! Wow..,' said Firan and looked away. The bus arrived and the conversation ended there.

In the class room everybody had to sit in their newly allotted place, the monitors ensured that. Firan did not talk to Feroz, but then she did not turn away either. Anyway, for most part of the day today they were supposed to be in the field for their preliminary matches and athletics. They had their sports day in the coming week. The band was practicing for the March Past. After the first four periods everybody had to assemble in the ground and participate in various events. There was a festive feeling. Even the first four classes were not held properly.

'There is just too much noise outside.' complained Mrs Anita.

Joyce smiled widely at that comment and looked around to share her thought. Anita ma'am caught the look and Joyce immediately buried her head inside her bag pretending to look for something.

All the students of the school were divided into four groups called houses for the purpose of extra curricular activities. They were named Blue, Green,

Red and Yellow house. The colour of the shirt indicated each student's house.

From the Eight Std Anaida and Bonty were leading the contingent of their houses Red and Blue respectively. It was lucky that they were sitting together. They sat and planned how they would make their teams win the 'Best March Past' trophy. Feroz and Ajay kept looking in Bonty's direction to get his attention but he seemed totally focused on Anaida. Most of the Eight Std students were in March Past. Feroz, Rahul, Priya and Joyce were good in athletics from their class.

A long bell signalled the practice time and everyone dashed off in different directions. They were well into the last half hour of the practice session when the PT Sir came rushing towards Feroz and told him that the Principal was calling him. Feroz sprinted off his mind working at double speed. *Have I done something wrong?* He tried to think.

As soon as he reached the door of the Principal's room. He stopped and brushed his hair, tucked his shirt and took a deep breath before entering. He asked 'May I come in Sir?'

'Come in,' said, the Principal, Mr. Jacob.

When he entered the Principal's office he found that there were some more students in the room. Firan was also there. Mr. Jacob looked at all of them and said

'I am pleased to announce that all of you, two from each class have been selected to represent our school in the science exhibition. You have one week to come up with an interesting project.'

Feroz and Firan were partners... again!

15
What's Wrong?

'Oh! So nice to see you, come in... come in.' said Firan's mother to Feroz.

'Umm...is Firan there aunty, I wanted to discuss some projects for our science exhibition' said Feroz.

'Oh, are you taking part in some exhibition?'

'Err... we both have been chosen from our class.'

Clearly Firan hadn't told her mother about it. He felt slightly awkward. Luckily Firan entered the room and said, 'Hi!'

'Firan' her mom said, 'he has come to discuss about the science exhibition... you both can go to your room, I will ask Leelabai to give you some ice cream.'

Both of them went up and soon Leelabai brought bowlful of ice cream. Feroz loved ice cream and picked it up immediately. He walked to the window and peered out; he could see his room window. He couldn't see the 'fallen ladder' and he blurted out 'Where is the ladder?'

The moment the sentence was out of his mouth he knew he had made a mistake. Firan was staring at him. Many questions passed her mind. *Had he seen her sneaking out? Or Oh my god! climbing back in? No, I would have seen him if he had watched me.*

Feroz stared back. *O god, what do I say now. She will again think that I was spying on her.*

There was pin drop silence, Firan finally asked

'How do you know about the ladder?'

'Um... I have been seeing it standing against your window for sometime now.... from my window........ when I was looking out, err....., one day,' he explained hopelessly.

'Are you spying on me?'

'What? No Firan'

'Come on........... First I catch you under the bushes peering into our garden, then I see you looking out of your window to see what I am doing in my garden while waiting for Mom and now I find you have been keeping tabs on me. What does all this mean?"

'Nothing, I mean, I am not spying on you, that garden episode was just coincidental... What about you, even you followed me into the shack?' spluttered Feroz realizing suddenly that he had actually been spying the past few days.

Silence hung in the air.

Feroz suddenly got the courage to come clear and divulged out everything.

'I saw a ladder placed against your window. It was so conspicuous; I thought perhaps you were planning to sneak out. I wanted to know where you were going. So I watched constantly, however I missed it,' Feroz stopped, seeing her glare.

'Yes, continue, Nosey Ferozy' she said

'What? What an awful name. Look, I think I will go home,' said Feroz

'Oh! No, you will not, finish your story first.'

'Why should I? You are being so rude.'

'Ok, I won't be rude Nosey Ferozy'

'Will you stop calling me by that name?'

'I'll try, no promise'

'Well, I saw you climb back up the ladder,' he suppressed a giggle and added, 'it was a funny sight.'

And suddenly he started laughing remembering some scene. Firan glared at first then her face suddenly softened. He continued to guffaw and laugh and control at the same time. Firan couldn't control herself and joined him and laughed out loud, punching him at the same time.

'You should have seen yourself, hanging on the win....'

And he couldn't stop and laughed again. Firan remembered how she had hung there and to think that Feroz had been watching all the time made her feel like laughing out more. She roared laughing

'What a sight I must have been!'

'You bet, especially when you literally scaled the wall'

And they laughed and laughed tears poured down their cheeks, but they still laughed uncontrollably.

Her Mom entered hearing all the laughter.

'What happened?' she asked

'Nothing,' said Firan immediately, 'Mom!'

She hated it when Mom just arrived like that.

'Ok, Ok I am out of here,' her Mom muttered and went out.

'That's not very kind,' remarked Feroz.

't's ok,' said Firan clamming up immediately.

'Think I will go now and thanks once again. Will catch up tomorrow, Bye,' he said and left

Pangs of remorse, grief and panic engulfed her, *why did she behave like how she did? What's wrong?* She tried to think of some valid reason for her behaviour, but there wasn't any. *Do I hate my Mom? Why did I behave so badly?*

A part of her mind said 'well, Mom should not have come in like that, she is so inquisitive all the time' and the other part of her mind knew that this was not true. She knew she had hurt her Mom and she should go and apologize. She turned towards the door and then turned back. She just couldn't do it.

She stayed in the room, her mind kept going back to the incident. *Feroz must be thinking that I am an awful person.* She didn't like that thought. *Why? What did it matter whatever Feroz thought of her?* She hated him, right? 'Wrong' said a part of her.

She felt confused the whole evening and didn't talk much at dinner time too. Her mother also didn't say anything at all. Back in her room she took out her diary and wrote

Dear Diary

I am feeling awful. What's wrong with me? I feel like crying.

Why is all this happening, Why was I rude to Mom especially in front of Feroz. Why does it matter to me what he thinks about me?

Oh! God, please help me. I know I said that I am never ever .....ever ....going to ask you anything... ever. I am sorry.

Feroz got back home in a solemn mood. He called up Bonty to cheer himself up but Bonty was not at home. Bonty's Mom told him that he had called his team for extra practice for the march past. He was really concentrating hard on winning that cup. In fact he was also studying very well these days, as they say totally focused and all.

He wondered if it had anything to do with Anaida. He then called Ajay. They chatted for sometime and then Ajay said his dad had just returned from work and didn't like him on the phone much.

'Bye, see you tomorrow' he said and put the phone down.

Ajay's parents considered everything other than studying a waste of time. Especially telephone conversations were totally 'useless' according to his dad. He had to take permission to call anybody. This irked him to no end. The consequence of all this restrictions was that he wanted the forbidden thing. He would talk endlessly when someone called him. He would pick up the phone as soon as his parents went out and chat for long hours. Today when he heard Ajay say 'I need to put the phone down' he felt Ajay was changing.

Feroz put the phone down and now felt that all of them were changing in some way or the other. There were signs. What happened to the idea of forming a club? The enthusiasm had died. It remained a nameless club.

He tried to then take out his books and read for the upcoming examination but he could not concentrate. Words floated meaninglessly making him dizzy and sleepy. Though he was reading, he registered nothing and finally gave up and fell asleep.

He woke up with a start the next day. He couldn't recollect when he fell asleep. He got ready, grabbed an apple and rushed out chewing it hard. While passing by Firan's house he saw her also rushing out. He could hear her Mom yell

'Did you finish your milk?'

This was the first time they had got out almost at the same time.

'Hi,' said Firan.

"Hi, same time first time!' remarked Feroz.

She nodded.

He chewed on noisily and said with his mouth full

'So, all ok with your Mom?'

Firan just shrugged and didn't say anything; they walked to the bus stop together.

He is cute and sensitive, Firan resolved... *maybe all boys are not crass.*

16
All Set

The whole school was in a 'sports day' mood and again not many classes were held. Everyone was busy with some activity or the other. Most of the classes were on self study basis. Teachers entered and asked the students to finish their pending work or study for their examination, which was scheduled a week after the sports day. As long as they maintained discipline and didn't make noise, teachers were happy doing their own work. Many students played naught and cross or book cricket, on the sly.

'So, where did you go that day, down the ladder?' whispered Feroz to Firan

'I went to my hideout,' she said, 'it seems silly now, but it was exciting.'

'Where is this hideout?' enquired Feroz

'Beyond, on the other side of the garden'

'Umm...all by yourself?'

'Of course, what did you think, idiot'

'What fun is that?'

'You won't know. Have you tried sneaking out?'

'No'

'You want to try?'

'I don't know'

'Are you scared?

'No'

'I am sure you are scared, why wouldn't you want to try sneaking out at night?'

'Umm .... Because there is no need and all creepy, crawly things come out at night, why disturb them?'

'Now I am sure you are scared.'

'I am not,' said Feroz, a bit too loudly and the teacher looked up and said

'Yes Feroz, What are you doing? Stop talking or should I say whispering '

Everyone looked in his direction and grinned.

Feroz scowled and took out his Maths book to do some sums.

'Let's go together one of the nights'

'Are you crazy? No'

'sh... shhh...' said the teacher

They didn't get a chance to talk much the rest of the day in the school. On the way back from the bus stop Firan again persisted.

'Don't you want to at least see the hideout? It is strange, you were so curious, now that you know, you are not interested. Funny!'

This made him think - *yeah so true, perhaps I should see the place. What is the harm anyway?* So he gave in and said 'Ok'

'I will call you and we will plan something' shouted Firan as she entered her house.

'Ok, bye' Feroz yelled back.

Firan's Mom was surprised when she said Hi! and rushed to change her uniform. 'Somebody is in a good mood today' Mrs Amir muttered. Firan came and sat down to eat, she was very chatty and told her Mom everything that happened in school that day, what fun they had with no studies. Her Mom listened with interest and she wanted to remind Firan of the examination round the corner but refrained.

Feroz also entered his own house and yelled 'Hi! Mom, what's for lunch?'

He opened the fridge and as usual gulped a bottle of cold water down. He also told his Mom what fun they had in school.

Firan called up later in the evening to chat.

'Let's plan,' she said promptly when he said 'hello'

'When can we sneak out?' she enquired

'Umm......,' was all he could say

'Are your parents going out any evening?'

'I'll have to find out,' he replied

'Ok, mine are going out on Friday evening err... that would be day after tomorrow, for a cultural evening at the Habitat Centre, we could go then.'

'Ok, we'll see, I don't think mine are going anywhere on Friday.'

'Listen, whenever it happens you need to be ready, you would need to carry a few things, write it down: a torch; a mat or something to sit on; a bottle of water and something to eat maybe.'

'Ok, do you think I should invite Bonty and Ajay?'

'Lets try it out first then we can plan a midnight picnic with our friends. What do you say?'

'Yeah, I think that is a good idea.'

'Ok,' said Firan

'Ok,' said Feroz

'Umm...bye' said Feroz again and put the phone down.

Next day in the school they hardly got any time to chat about it. Feroz was in the finals of the 200m race and the 400m race, and so he needed to practice. Mrs Anita ma'am had requested Firan and Joyce to do up their bulletin board outside their class room with the 'sport day' as the theme. By the time the school got over they were totally drained and didn't talk at all on the way back.

The plan turned into action sooner than expected. Feroz thought it would be quite sometime before both their parents would go out at the same time. But as it happened even his parents were planning to go for the same cultural show. In fact both the families were planning to go together.

'Now that you are friends, maybe you can do your home work together and have dinner together' suggested his Mom.

As soon as Firan came to know about this new development she called him.

'Yes, yes, yes' she exclaimed as soon as Feroz picked up the phone. It was so typical of her to start off like that without even saying a hello or hi, and he was beginning to feel her enthusiasm, it was infectious.

'So... What now? How do we go about it?' he asked

'Simple, we tell them we have a test and we are going to study together here, at my house. As soon as they leave we also leave,' she said with excitement

'Ok'

'Tomorrow we will have to plan everything in the school. There isn't much time left. The cultural program starts at 7pm. So our parent's will probably leave at 6pm. It will end at around 9pm I think and then there is dinner for all the invitees. So they won't be home before 11pm. You can come as soon as they leave.'

'Ok'

'Hello, don't you have anything to add?'

'Can't think of anything, you have thought of everything' and he japed at her by saying, 'you also have a lot of experience in all this stuff.'

'Very funny, ok, we will do rest of the planning in school tomorrow, bye'

Phew, this girl is one big planner. Feroz wished he could share all this with Ajay and Bonty but these days they hardly had any time to talk. He lay in his bed thinking about the way they would sneak out at night. He had never done such a thing ever before. He felt very excited.

17
9.25

'Come on, Feroz are you ready? Pick up your bag and please no wasting time, finish your home work and if you have time you can start doing some revision work with Firan, Hurry up,' said his Mom.

Mr. and Mrs Shah were supposed to pick Col and Mrs Amir. When they reached their house all three of them were standing outside. Feroz got off quickly and wished Firan's parent.

'Congratulations, I believe you have also been selected for the science exhibition' remarked Firan's dad.

'Thank you,' beamed Feroz.

'Bye!' they yelled and waved as the car moved away.

'We will wait for 10min or so, lest they come back to get something,' said Firan

Both of them went inside the house. Firan went up and brought down a bag. She then went into the kitchen took out some aluminium foils, cling films and zip-locks. Then she called him to the dinning table where the food was laid.

'Pack the stuff that you would like to eat in these,' she said pointing the foils etc.

There was a delicious looking biryani, some yummy paranthas, koftas and raita. Both of them got busy carefully spooning ladleful of food into the foils and zip locks. All this took them nearly half an hour.

Firan then put the packets, two plates and several spoons and a bottle of water in yet another bag. She checked her set of house keys and asked 'Shall we go?'

Feroz nodded.

She looked at her watch it was nearly 7pm. They got out and carefully locked the front door. It was a full moon night and there was plenty of light. The street lights were on, they could make out the way very easily. Slowly they walked towards the hideout.

Firan walked a little ahead showing the way. Feroz was surprised to see so many trees and bushes here. He had never noticed this, not even from his window. A lemony waft made his stomach rumble. He was already feeling hungry but they had to finish their home work first which reminded him that he wasn't carrying a torch or a candle. He stopped and asked Firan 'Do we need to get some candles or something.'

'I have got an emergency light—fully charged,' replied Firan.

Suddenly she took a right turn and went under a huge bush, scrambling on his fours he followed suit. When he came out on the other side he could immediately see the hideout, it looked exactly like how she had explained. He looked around, how beautiful it looked, and then he turned back to look at Firan's house. It was not in sight. He had to stand on his toes to see it and even then he couldn't see it clearly.

'So what do you think? Enquired Firan

'Nice'

They walked a little ahead towards the tree which had thick surface root forming a nice place to sit.

'It's a bit strange that there should be so many trees here,' said Feroz, 'Do you know what is on the other side?'

'No, I only got so far,' she replied.

'Let me see, I think it should go and meet the back lane of Arjun Vihar. Let's finish everything fast and go check out.'

'Yes, Finally! You are suggesting something exciting.'

They spread the mats and took their math homework. Between both of them, they were able to finish it in no time. Next they had to write some question and answers in History, which took some time -- History madam's love for long answers. After they finished their history work, they felt relaxed and took out the food, and started eating. Things got a little messy.

'We should have brought all these things in boxes and eaten from it. Your Mom cooks very well, everything is so tasty. So, what did you do all alone over here, the last time you came?' asked Feroz

'You know what, there was this cat.....' and explained the whole vanishing act that this cat did.

'Really?'

'Yeah, it just disappeared; there was something eerie about it.....'

Something unexplainable tugged his heart, maybe it was the atmosphere or the fact that he had bottled up his thoughts about the weird happenings past few weeks. He poured out the snake and the cat incident he had witnessed the night before Sir had brought the snake to class.

Firan listened awestricken. After a few minutes of silence she said, 'Batra Sir is quite intriguing...'

Feroz rolled his eyes and exclaimed 'Yeah...'

'That cat kept looking at me and following me...... do you think it is the same cat? I wonder why it looked at me like that as if it wanted to talk to me...' remarked Firan.

A soft breeze started blowing; they continued to sit silently for a while each lost in thoughts.

Finally Firan couldn't contain herself and also came forth with the murmur that she thought she had heard.

'Twas as if somebody was talking far...far... away'

'From which direction did it come? Asked Feroz

'That is the strangest part; it was coming with a slight breeze, from no particular direction.'

'Oh...'

Elsewhere Yapra was feeling elated, he was in complete tune with Firan and Feroz. He ensured that their mind did not discuss him at all. He was mildly afraid that his name might trigger some reaction in their brains and they might abandon the rest of the plan.

Soon Feroz suggested that they should start exploring before it got too late. They put everything into the bags and placed them between two low wedges on the root. They decided not to take the emergency light because it was quite cumbersome to handle and the full moon was providing enough light. Firan put off the emergency light and checked her watch. It was 9.25pm. They still had plenty of time.

'I hope there are no snakes. 'Did you see any snakes here?'

'No' replied Firan

'Don't worry; we will deal with it when we come across one.' She added, 'maybe this path will just lead us straight to the road.'

'Yes that I think I am sure of. My sense of direction says so.'

They started walking away from the hideout and Firan's house. There were more trees; Feroz was amazed to see this. *How come there is so much of vegetation here?* Little more ahead high and prickly bushes obstructed their route.

'I suggest we try and go in a straight line from the hideout. We will save time on our way back,' suggested Firan.

So they kept going straight, scrambling under bushes, bending under low branches, in the darkness it seemed as if they had gone quite far from their hide out, but when they turned to see, they could still see the top branches of the hideout tree. Feroz was going ahead now, he kept feeling, beyond this bush, the road will definitely be there, but once he crossed it, more trees and more bushes appeared. He finally asked

'How long have we been walking?'

Firan looked at her watch it showed 9.25pm.

'What?' exclaimed Firan 'I think my watch has stopped; I know we started walking at 9.25pm.' She peered at her watch again. Feroz looked at his.

'It is 9.25pm now,' he said, 'You must not have seen it correctly earlier.'

Firan saw that her watch was working the seconds hand's was moving alright! *Perhaps I had not seen it properly.*

They walked for some more time with Firan leading now. There were many trees with very low branches. It soon got very tiring bending under each of them. They stopped and looked back to see if they could see the hideout tree.

'Err... is it that one?' Asked Feroz

Firan looked at the many tree tops visible now. She couldn't make out which one was their tree. She looked at Feroz and said 'I don't know.'

Their eyes met, and Feroz saw some panic in her eyes. So he reassured her and said, 'don't worry, we have been coming in a straight line we can always go back, anyway the road can't be far now.'

He started walking ahead and said just to make conversation 'You know maybe we should have carried our bags. We could have taken the road route back.'

He looked at this huge thick bush and thought this must be it and quickly scrambled under it. A surprise was waiting for them on the other side.

18
Rustle

Feroz emerged from under the bush and stood up and Firan quickly followed him and stood right next to him. Both of them gaped at what was in front of them. They had expected to see a road but what they found was a very low bridge. They could see a dirt path going under the bridge, there was thick vegetation and growth on either side of the bridge. Beyond the bridge, the growth was even thicker, though the path was clearly leading somewhere.

They were totally at loss and stood inert for sometime – unable to decide. Finally, Firan asked

'What's this?'

'Don't know'

'Could it be that there is a village or something behind the back lane of Arjun Vihar,' she suggested.

'Never heard of it,' he replied, 'What do we do now, go ahead or go back?'

Firan looked at her watch. If they had time they could go ahead else she felt it would be better to go back. She pressed the light button of her watch to see the time and it showed 9.25. She brought it closer and fumbled with it for sometime when she heard Feroz say

'Come on decide...what's the time?'

'9.25' she replied quietly.

'What?' he said, 'let me see,' and he looked at his watch indeed it was 9.25. It was ticking there was no doubt about that the seconds were ticking positively.

'Why is the time not going beyond 9.25 in both our watches?' he asked

'I have no idea, it's creepy,' she said and looked at him.

He looked back at her. *These things didn't happen in the real world. They happened in story books. Strange things happened to him alright, but he was quite convinced that 'his overactive mind' made up some part of it. But then, how come now even with Firan it was happening? Am I asleep and dreaming?* Wondered Feroz

At the same time Firan started to think – *is something bizarre happening? Am I dreaming? It is as if the time is standing still. Does it really mean that it is 9.25 only?*

'I suggest we go ahead,' she said and added, 'I am sure the road will appear sooner or later; we can then ask for some help from someone in Arjun Vihar. I will pick the books and the bags later in the morning. What do you say?'

'Hmm.., ok seems like a good plan,' he replied while thinking, *here I am imagining stupid things and Firan is making concrete plans.*

They started walking ahead and reached the bridge. As they walked under it an unusual sensation passed through both of them, though neither mentioned it to the other. A feeling of warmth followed by a feeling of cold and a kind of lightness in the head followed by heaviness, spread through their bodies, but the moment they cleared the bridge the sensation disappeared.

They started walking again, now going together. The path was just wide enough for two people to walk. They kept looking left and then right, left and then right, hoping to catch a glimpse of a road or some street light or anything familiar. Slowly they entered into what looked like a jungle of trees, shrubs, creepers and vines.

'A place like this in the heart of Delhi? It's unbelievable,' muttered Feroz.

He kept looking around wishing that he had brought a torch along. Surprisingly they were able to see the path clearly as if the moon was directing all its light on just the path and nothing else. All around it was very dark. Their eyes were totally accustomed to the darkness. They kept walking. Soon their legs started to ache.

'I am sure we have been walking for nearly an hour or so since we crossed the bridge.'

'Yes, definitely an hour,' she replied looking at her watch again. It still showed 9.25

Suddenly they heard a rustle and they stopped on track. Both of them looked at each other. Firan gave a questioning look. Feroz shrugged his shoulders in reply.

They stood still, both holding their breath as if breathing would mean noise. Another rustle sent a chill down their spine. This time it seemed closer. They looked all around they could make out the tree trunks, outline of bushes, they could see the path where they were standing, but they could not see the ground where the bushes and trees were growing. Anything could be there making that sound. Some dry leaves crackled, a soft breeze started to blow. The breeze brought a peculiar smell of vegetation and the smell of rot. It was a strong smell, but not the kind where you want to hold your nose, another unexplainable kind.

They looked at each other again. Firan's mouth was dry, she swallowed some saliva to moisten her throat and to whisper something, but she couldn't think of anything to say. Another rustle made them come closer and stand absolutely still.

'I think it is a snake,' Feroz whispered into her ears.

She nodded. They waited like that for sometime; the next rustle did not come. Has 'whatever it is' moved away or is it waiting for them to move. Both were unable to decide. Feroz whispered into her ears again, 'Shall we go ahead?'

She nodded again. Just as they were about to take a step, they heard the rustle again and the mild breeze brought the smell again and they stopped and stood still. Goose bumps appeared all over and blood drained from their faces. They were very scared.

A dark form seemed to move towards them. It looked like the shadow of a huge man. Tears welled in their eyes. A breeze blew and they were shocked to see the shadow move and wave as if it were made of something light. As if it was a cloth on the clothesline moving in the breeze. They did not dare to move and watched it mesmerized.

It moved effortlessly, its movement was followed by the sound of rustling leaves and the vague smell. It came closer and closer towards them, the smell now unbearable. Firan felt vomit come to her mouth, she wanted to retch, and her stomach was in a spasm. Feroz had the same feeling. Both of them however did not move they had their eyes glued on the shadow.

The shadow melted into the darkness after sometime. They continued to stand still for a long time. Their legs ached, they felt tired. *What's happening? What have we got into?*

'Mom and dad would be back by now, I think,' whispered Firan.

'It's been a while since we heard the last rustling, shall we try going ahead?' asked Feroz

'Ok,' she replied.

Feroz moved one step ahead and stopped, nothing happened. He took another step, all was quiet – no movement. He caught Firan's hand and signed with the other hand to walk softly. They moved ever so slowly trying not even to breath freely. Nothing happened. Encouraged they picked a little speed and walked faster away from the spot.

Once out of that area they became more courageous, and wanting to end this episode, they started running. They ran and ran and ran, and soon started noticing that the trees were becoming fewer and the surrounding area was getting clearer. They continued to run covering a lot of ground, a big bush appeared again in front of them, they scrambled again and came out on the other side and saw a tunnel. Without stopping they went into the tunnel, it was darker than outside but way up ahead they could faintly see the other end.

They continued running and when they approached the other end they noticed that they had to go up a gradual climb which was strange since they hadn't gone down-slope anywhere during their journey. The moment they stepped out of the tunnel they had to mask their eyes with their hands because it was so bright.

The sun was shining brightly. Their eyes had become so used to the darkness that the sudden light was hurting them. Feroz tried to open his eyes and look around, but his eyes started watering immediately, he closed it again. It was just too too bright.

'Have we reached the road? Have we walked all night?' asked Feroz

'Looks like it,' said Firan.

She had her hand over her eyes and was trying to see from the gaps between her fingers.

There was a vast expanse of land with dry grass all over. Very few trees were standing here and there. A shade was forming under a tree close-by. Firan caught hold of Feroz, who still had his eyes closed, and pulled him under the tree. Under the shade of the tree they were able to somewhat open their eyes. Feroz looked around.

'So, where are we?' asked Firan

'Never seen this place, I have never seen so much of empty space with no buildings in Delhi--ever'

'Look,' said Firan pointing at a hill towards their left.

'We can go on top of that and see where we are.'

'Yes, let's go,' and they raced towards the hill.

19
Zoned

All along Yapra had been following them closely not physically but mentally. He was taken aback when the children encountered the shadow form because he had imagined himself to be huge shadow following them. How his imagination was taking a real form he did not understand. But the moment he realized this he let go of the thought and rightfully the form disappeared from the children's sight.

When they entered the tunnel he started losing sight of them. He concentrated hard; he created the tunnel for them to enter this other world. It was under his control so why was he losing their sight. Yapra started to grapple in his mind and suddenly the children disappeared when they left the tunnel and entered the other world.

Feroz and Firan reached all the way up the hill panting and puffing, tired to the core, their bones ached and they started feeling thirsty too. As soon as they reached the top they panned their eyes.

'Look! A house,' shouted Firan pointing again towards the left and said, 'Thank god! Just when I was thinking all these bizarre thoughts, it's a village!'

'I can't see any more houses, this is weird. I think we need to be careful. How can some one live so secluded? ... Look around, there is absolutely nothing as far as the eyes can see on either side,' said Feroz

Firan's enthusiasm took a beating when she understood the gravity of the fact that a single house in the middle of nowhere was mysterious.

'We don't have a choice... we have to approach that house and ask anyone who is there if they can help us get back home,' said Firan, 'Mom and dad are going to be very angry with me'

'I can't imagine how upset my parents are going to be.'

They started walking towards the house. Going down slope was easier than climbing up. Midway they stopped when they saw a figure come out of the house and potter around. The figure suddenly looked up in their direction and started walking towards them.

There was something oddly familiar about the way the figure moved.

'Is it someone we know?' asked Firan

'I think so,' replied Feroz.

The figure waved.

And both of them waved back. This was the first pleasant site that they experienced since they had started walking.

As they got closer, it became clearer to Feroz that the figure was their Science Sir, Mr. Batra, *'Prof Moody' to be precise.* He was surprised. Sir also recognized Feroz and Firan and said 'You?' It was not very clear whether he was unhappy to find that it was them or whether he was surprised to see them.

'Oh! Hello Sir,' said Firan feebly.

'What are you both doing here? Firstly how did you get here?' asked Mr. Batra.

'We ...err...,' Feroz started to say when he realized how absurd everything would sound, their sneaking out and all the events that followed. He wiped his continually watering eyes taking time to reply.

'Sir, Can you help us get back home we have lost our way,' said Firan without even thinking for a second.

How does she do that? Wondered Feroz, *and it comes so easily to her. And how appropriately she had asked for help without giving away much.*

'No, I can't help you,' said Batra Sir and he stood looking lost and confused.

Feroz and Firan looked at each other. Firan started thinking, *why did he say that? Why is he looking so confused?* Suddenly they heard him say 'follow me' and off he went towards his house.

Both of them followed half running as Sir was walking just too fast. He was going in the direction of the building from where he had seen them. As they got closer they could see that the building was made of some type of big black sparkling smooth stones. The door was cream coloured, made of some kind of aluminium and plastic mix. The windows had frames which were made of the same material as the door, but there were no glasses or grills so it was a kind of hole in the wall. They could see the curtains hanging, partly drawn

They felt a wave of relief as soon as they entered the house. Light streamed through the window hole and the open door but it was no longer so bright. Their eyes relaxed and stopped watering. They found that it was not a regular house, this house had just one huge hall, each corner of the room had things that would go into a particular room, like one corner had bedding on the floor, another corner had all the kitchen counter and a basin with one tap, the third corner had a low chair and many books strewn around. In the centre there were few low stools, few low tables, lanterns, and some rugs. There was another door near the fourth corner. There were cupboards made of the same material as the door, cream coloured.

Batra Sir went and got some water for them in two small earthen glasses. They gulped it down, it tasted fresh and cool, Sir poured some more and they gulped that too. Then he abruptly said, 'sit, sit and tell me how you came here, tell me everything'

Feroz and Firan looked at each other. Sir, with all his jerky movements, was scaring them. They were feeling completely exhausted with this adventure of theirs. For one thing they were not able to comprehend head or tail of what was happening. Both of them felt they were dreaming all this. Batra Sir's voice brought them to reality. This was no dream.

'Tell me, how did you find this place? Repeated Batra Sir

'What place is this?' asked Firan

'Where are we?' added Feroz

Looking at both their faces, which had become very small; Batra Sir realized that they were tired. He had to quell his curiosity and let them rest first and then he would question them later and get all the information out.

'I think both of you are very tired, I suggest you sleep for sometime. We can discuss this matter after a couple of hours of rest. Would you like to....'

'What is the time?' interrupted Firan

'It's... err, I think you should sleep on the mattress over there and Feroz, you can sleep on this thick rug here.' He said and then he walked out of the room.

Both of them looked at each other and Firan asked with lifted eyebrows what to make of all this. Feroz shrugged, he couldn't handle this anymore, he took out the rug shook it and spread it properly and decided to crash out. Firan did the same, mumbling 'maybe we will wake up at home.'

Feroz woke up with a start and looked at his watch, it was showing 6 O'clock. He was relieved; *my watch has started working, now everything will be normal.* He looked around, he was still lying on the rug; Firan was still asleep on the mattress. *If it was 6 O'clock then it must be early morning. They had probably walked all through the night, his parents didn't know where he was, and they would be so worried. How did he get into all this?* Then he suddenly recollected it had been very bright when they had reached Batra Sir's house, *so was it evening now - 6pm? Nothing is normal,* he felt dizzy...

Batra Sir was making something in the kitchen corner and a pleasant lemony aroma was spreading. He got into sitting position and looked around; he needed to go to the bathroom. His movement made Sir turn around. Sir asked 'Are you feeling rested?'

Feroz nodded

'You can go freshen up there' he said pointing at the door near the fourth corner.

He went through it and found a covered corridor leading to another door. He went ahead and opened it. It was a bathroom alright; very big and spacious, it was also made of the same smooth stones. Even the pot was made of the smooth stone, it was very clean.

There was a stone basin with one tap. In one corner there were a stack of three buckets and few mugs all cream coloured and made of the same material as the door and the window frame.

Feroz washed his face thinking what an unusual house this was. *Somehow I have to quickly get back home,* and with that determination he went back to the hall. Sir was setting the same earthen glasses on a small table in the centre of the room. Feroz went towards him and sat down on the stool. Sir handed him the glass. Feroz took it and smelt it, it was refreshing so he took a sip, and it tasted sweet and sour and salty, but he liked it. They didn't talk at all. Feroz was contemplating to ask a question when Firan sat up with a start just like he had. She looked at both of them and stood up immediately.

'The bathroom is on that side if you want to freshen up,' said Sir.

Firan went, opened, then peered and disappeared behind it.

'Sir..umm...,' Feroz started to say when Sir raised his hand stopping him.

'Before you say or ask anything I want to tell you something. Let Firan come back.'

Feroz nodded and started sipping his drink. Firan returned after sometime and joined them. Sir gave her a glass too.

'Listen, I don't know how I am going to explain this but it is really surprising to see you here on this side.' Sir paused and continued, 'this Zone is blocked and nobody from the other side can come on this side unless you have the permissions...' Looking at their bewildered faces he again continued 'I know I am not making any sense...but here is a deal if you tell me everything and I mean everything about your journey to this place, then I will tell you more about this place.'

The effect of Yapra's control was starting to wear out in the Zone. The children felt lost and confused.

20
Tunnel?

'Sir, we just want to go home. Our parents will be worried. I am sure my dad would have called the police by now. We don't want to know what this place is, just help us get back,' said Feroz.

'I can't help you unless I know how you got here, I don't know the way out for both of you,' Sir replied.

'What do you mean, you come to school everyday!' said Firan.

'I said... I don't know the way out for... **You both,**' He specified.

Sir was acting all mysterious and it was frightening both of them. Firan felt that this had gone too far, *it was better to explain the whole episode and be done with it.* So she started narrating the whole episode, Feroz joined her and between both of them they told everything, how Firan found the 'Hideout', how they planned an evening out there, how they started exploring, found the bridge, how their watches were ticking yet not going beyond 9.25, the thick vegetation, the path... the tunnel.... everything came out.

Sir listened to the whole story without interrupting even once. In the end when both of them fell silent he said, 'We refer to this place as 'The Zone.' From where you are coming we call it the 'Other side'. When I say we, I mean those who live here. We are a group of twenty four people six each of scientists, environmentalists, science teachers and doctors. Only we live here in this vast zone. We have created this and we love it here, it's our country, our world, our earth. I am sure you want to ask many questions, who, why, what, when etc. In time I might need to answer all those. But what I want to say right now is that we have so designed and safeguarded this Zone that no one can enter or exit without our combined permission, I mean you need permission from each one of us. So your arriving here is a complete mystery because I know I didn't give you the permission. Have you met anyone who said you could enter the Zone or has anyone shared this story with you, do you know about this place?'

They shook their heads. They were both fascinated by the narrative. There was silence. They both were trying to digest all this information that Sir had just provided.

'Will you take me through the route you came?' asked Sir breaking the silence.

They looked at each other; they didn't want to go back the same route. It was tiring and they didn't want to go back through those trees and bushes again. But it seemed like they didn't have a choice.

'This time I will be there,' Sir said looking at their worried faces.

They nodded.

'Oh! Do you want to eat or drink something?'

Surprisingly both of them felt full. They had had only a glass of that drink Sir had given. 'I am feeling full,' both said together

'Great, let's go,' said Sir and went out.

Sir rushed on.

Both of them followed him and the moment they were out through that door they had to cover their eyes with their hands again. It was blazing bright. They looked down and moved their hands slowly away from their eyes. Their eyes smarted a bit and watered.

They wiped the water away and blinked several times making their eyes water more. It took some time before they were able to look up. Sir was way ahead, already half way up the hill.

'Why is it so bright here? What do you think of all this?' asked Feroz.

'Right now it is not making any sense; I am hoping that all this is a dream. When we came at that time also it was so bright, does it mean that we have slept through a whole day and a whole night? ... and now, we are going out at the same time that we came?'

'I have no idea, it seems impossible that we could have slept for 24 hours!'

They hurried towards Sir, who had by now reached the top. When they reached the top they looked towards the right, to spot the tree under which they had stood and seen this hill. There was only one tree close to the hill and they reasoned that must be the one. They started going towards it and reached it easily.

'The tunnel should be here,' said Firan. Her eyes started to water again, and she had to keep wiping her eyes and Feroz narrowed his into a small split, to avoid watering.

There was no tunnel.... there were shrubs and tall grasses, but no tunnel. All three of them spread out a little and combed the place. The tunnel had vanished, it wasn't there! Firan and Feroz back tracked, discussing how they came out from an opening, and had immediately masked their face, how they had run for cover from the bright sun, but the spot that they kept going back to, had no tunnel opening or even a hole in the ground. They looked at each other unable to believe it. How can a whole tunnel go missing?

'Its not here...Where has the tunnel gone?' Firan exclaimed spinning round and round.

Both of them looked at Batra Sir and he said, 'let us just try again, perhaps it wasn't near this tree, let's try around that one, a little further away. It must be somewhere; we may be looking in the wrong place.'

So they went ahead next to another tree. There was nothing there too. Firan and Feroz were both sure that this was not the place. They knew it was futile to look here. It had to be there where they were looking earlier.

'Hmm... , let's go home' said Sir suddenly and turned around and started going towards the hill, both of them quickly followed, eager to get inside the house and away from so much of brightness.

'Why is it so bright,' they asked running beside Sir.

'Is it?' asked Sir. When they both didn't reply he continued

'We will need to examine your eyes I am not sure how you entered the Zone and are able to see the details.'

Feroz was tired of mysterious replies so he asked 'What time is it?'

'Whatever time your watch is showing,' remarked Sir.

'It's showing 10 O'clock.'

'Then 10 it is my boy,' said Sir and hurried on.

'But...,' said Firan, and she couldn't complete the sentence as Sir was walking so fast.

They reached the house and Sir removed his shoes and put it against the wall. Both of them did the same.

'There is a meeting scheduled at 12 noon. We meet every Saturday and Sunday to discuss our experiments, outcomes and ideas. Those who need their quota of permissions also collect them on these days. So today being Saturday we are meeting. The venue is a place called 'Concurrence.' It's 'bout half an hours walk from here. Obviously I will have to take you both. I don't know what the Nouses will say, oh! By the way we call ourselves 'Nous' and not 'people.'

If it was Saturday noon then hell must have broken in their houses and frantic search operations would be in full swing by now. A whole lot of questions arose in their heads and they wanted the answers to them. However both of them remained silent.

'Would you like to freshen up before the meeting?' asked Sir.

'Sir, I want to clarify about certain things,' said Feroz.

'Go ahead, I know you are totally flummoxed, I will clarify as clearly as possible.'

'Sir, what is the time right now? At what time did we arrive? Asked Feroz

'How long did we sleep?' added Firan

'The time is exactly what your watches are showing which is..' he looked at his watch and said '10.30 a.m. You reached here a little after mid night and you must have slept for about five hours.'

'But it was so bright when we came out of the tunnel' exclaimed Firan

'Oh! Was it? Maybe you need your eyes examined'

This reply left them stumped.

When Sir didn't hear another question from them he said, 'we have half an hour to get ready, I will make something for you to eat meanwhile you can wash your faces and get ready. I know you have no fresh clothes, but you have to manage. One of you can help me peel these potatoes while the other gets ready.'

Though this was a strange place, they were glad that Sir was around to explain things.

One thing was clear they were in no danger ...or so they felt.

21
Nous Meeting

Feroz decided to get ready first and he went towards the only bathroom. Firan went beside Sir and started peeling the potatoes. Sir quickly made some rice and dal. Feroz returned and had to help Sir make the sabji and clear up the room. Then they kept the food on a table in the centre of the room.

'You both can have your food while I freshen up; all this is for you.'

And he went away.

Both of them were dying to talk to each other in private. 'A strange place, this is......,' began Firan.

'Where do you think the tunnel disappeared?' Feroz asked

'No idea, I am sure we were looking for it at the right place. Do you think somebody covered up the opening?'

Feroz shrugged and added, 'Sir is weird, if all of this food is for us. What will he eat?

'You are thinking of food.... wh...at about all the rest of the stuff? Look at this house!'

'I am not talking only about food, I was just saying in general; stop behaving as if you are the only smart one around here.'

'What did I say?' she said looking daggers at him.

 They ate quietly.

All this seemed improbable, but now they were convinced that it was really happening. This was no dream. Somehow they had entered this Zone.

They had to just wait and see what happened next and when they get an opportunity to try and go back to the other side. The things that were happening here were clearly a bit far fetched and seemed impossible --!'

They left the house at 11.25 a.m., again their eyes filled up with water when they stepped out. They looked down most of the way and quickly followed Sir. Both of them stole a glance now and then, there was nothing all around, no buildings or houses or even small shops, it was just vast stretches of land with some trees, shrubs and grass. After about 15min they could make out the shape of a building far ahead. Keeping it in site they walked straight towards it.

'Concurrence' was oval in shape and it was made of the same type of stones with which Sir's house was made, however these shone very brightly, giving it an almost white sheen in the sun. There was a flight of steps made of rocks and boulders leading up. At the top of the steps there was a corridor which seemed to be running all around the building and then there was an inner corridor which also seemed to be running all around the building. Beyond the corridor they could see an opening which was the way into the building; there were no doors or windows. All of them went through this opening.

Inside there was a huge oval table, again made of the same stones. The roof was covered with a transparent sheet allowing a lot of light to stream through. Five Nouses were already seated. Sir went towards them saying 'hullo hullo..' When they saw Feroz and Firan, they looked surprised and one of them said, 'who are these two? I haven't given permission to anyone'

'I don't know how these two have come here; they have an interesting story to tell. It would be better if we wait for everyone to assemble and then listen to these two,' said Sir.

By 12 dot everybody was seated, nearly all of them had raised their eyebrows when they saw Firan and Feroz and Sir kept repeating --

'I don't know how these two have come here; they have an interesting story to tell. It would be better if we wait for everyone to assemble and then listen to these two.'

All of them sat facing each other. Nobody sat at the head of the table.

Sir started by saying 'Since I brought these two, let me start. This is Feroz and that is Firan. I saw them at around quarter to one, early morning. Obviously I was surprised and confused. I brought them to my house and we talked about their fascinating journey to this place, after some rest I asked them to show me the way through which they had come. We went back to the place and they couldn't find the tunnel, through which they entered this Zone,' he turned and asked, 'Can I request you both to narrate the whole story again for the benefit of the Nouses here?'

Both of them repeated the story again. All the Nouses heard them without interrupting. They ended the story by saying that they couldn't find the tunnel today.

'This could be a very serious matter provided these two are telling the truth,' one of them said solemnly.

'Why would they be lying, Nina?' asked Sir.

Nina shrugged her shoulders.

'It's exactly how it happened, we are not lying,' said Firan. 'We want to go home; our families would be very worried. Please all of you just give us permission; we don't want to be here.'

Totally ignoring her, another Nous asked, 'does this mean that there is an entry to the Zone that we are not aware of?

'Naga, Looks like it, or maybe someone knows and is keeping a tab on us and these kids accidently discovered the route to this place. Did any thing else happen while you were exploring, anything unusual?' asked Nina

'Umm.. I did feel a bit woozy while crossing the bridge...,' Feroz started to say

'A feeling of warmth followed by a feeling of cold?' asked Firan

'Yes, yes ... did you also feel it and there was a kind of dizziness and then a weighing down feeling.'

'Yes, I too felt it, why didn't you tell me?' asked Firan

'For the same reason you didn't,' relied Feroz.

Firan scowled at him.

'What?' asked Feroz gesturing with his hands.

All the Nouses looked at each other.

'I suspect someone is playing games with us, they have already breached the Zone and maybe know about us.'

'I second what Aman is saying,' said Sir.

Everybody seemed to agree with this notion.

'We also saw a...,' said Firan and stopped.

'Yes, what?' asked Nina.

'A kind of shadow ... it was floating in the air, maybe making a lot of rustling noise, and a weird smell followed ...,' said Firan, sounding pathetic.

'I am unable to understand, what did you see, a man, animal, what?' said Aman.

'We are not sure, I think it was a shadow fluttering in the breeze with a vague smell,' said Feroz.

Everybody looked at them gravely and suddenly two Nouses got up, came towards them, and handcuffed them. Firan and Feroz were shocked and they stood up and looked at Sir, distraught.

'Riya and Riyaaz,' Sir said pointing at the two who had handcuffed them 'will take you to Decontam room. Just cooperate and you will come to no harm.'

Feroz noticed that Riya and Riyaaz were both wearing gloves and they had a bag each which they had slung across their shoulder so that the bag itself was in front near their left thigh... Riyaaz led Feroz with the chain attached to the handcuffs and Riya led Firan away from the room.

Even before they left the room, the Nouses started discussing amongst themselves.

'I think we should call it crisis and shut the Zone, no entry or exit till matters are resolved,' suggested Naga.

An enraged Firan turned and shouted 'what? No, you have to let us go and then you can shut it or whatever you want to do. Just let us go!'

Her hands were jerked and they were led away firmly.

22
Decontam

Riya and Riyaaz took them along the inner corridor behind the oval room. There were many corridors all leading to different rooms. There was a room marked First Room, they were made to sit there. Inside they could see another Oval Room and there was a wooden board with the word 'DECONTAM' written on it.

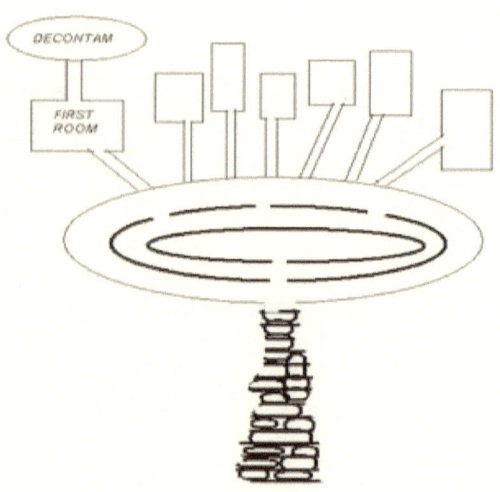

Riya and Riyaaz went off inside the 'Decontam' room. 'What now?' Firan whispered.

Feroz didn't feel like replying and cursed himself for making friends with this girl. *How nice my life had been and now it was a complete mess.* He felt angry and blurted out

'I wish I hadn't agreed to this plan of yours.... of seeing your hide out especially when my parents weren't around.'

She scowled at him.

At the same time Riya and Riyaaz came and took them inside. It was very dark; it took a while for their eyes to get accustomed. They were pushed into what looked like a transparent box through an opening and then the opening was closed by a shutter. They were totally trapped inside; their hand cuffs remained on them. Riya and Riyaaz stood outside watching them.

'What is going to happen now?' asked Firan in a worried voice.

'We will come back after two hours and take you out. You can do whatever you want, sit, stand, lay down even sleep, which I think is the best thing to do,' said Riyaaz.

'Meanwhile various methods will be adopted to decontaminate you both. Spraying, fumigation, hot air cold air, humidification and other such means. It might be irritating but it is a painless process,' said Riya.

'What are we being decontaminated for?' asked Firan.

'A whole lot of germs... which might have been implanted by the vague smelling breeze that you inhaled,' replied Riya and then they both left.

Feroz sat down against one of the sides of the Box. Firan sat down on the opposite side.

Firan felt that it was unfair that Feroz should hold her responsible for all this. Suddenly warm air started circulating in the box. This scared her, tears pricked her eyes, and she wanted to talk to Feroz to ease her feelings but decided not to. She brought her knees close to her chin and put her hands around her knees and rested her head on her knees. Suddenly she missed her Mom and prayed, *'I miss you Mom, please make all this disappear and make life normal again.'*

Feroz felt the warm air and gulped, he was scared. He curled and lay down on his side and closed his eyes willing all this to come to an end.

The warm air steadily became warmer and warmer and soon it became quite hot. This process made them both sweat a lot and soon their clothes were almost wet. Neither moved much. Then the heat reduced and slowly it was just warm. This process happened three times. Then it started to get cloudy inside the box as if some gas was being pumped inside, it was odourless and tasteless. Firan tried to see from where all this was coming inside the box. There were no inlets, no nozzles or sprinkler holes anywhere inside the box. It seemed as if all this was happening from somewhere right in the middle of the box. Slowly it became so dense that she couldn't even see Feroz on the opposite side. Just as it had begun the process reversed and then it became clear, and this again happened three times. Then a gas that was slightly pungent was released inside the box and in this way the pungent cycle began. Then there was a sweet smelling cycle, then cold air cycle, then another type of gas which made them very drowsy. Both of them slept off and they were totally unaware of the several stronger cycles that followed.

When Feroz opened his eyes he felt disoriented, he looked around and saw Firan, and that brought him to reality. He noticed that the shutter was up. He got up slowly; his body ached as if he had done a lot of physical activity. He went towards Firan and woke her up. She got up with a start and looked around and saw Feroz standing and looking at the open shutter. She too stood up slowly and they both got out and went into the waiting room.

Riya and Riyaaz were there and they immediately stood up.

'You both were sleeping so we did not wake you up. Decontam got over about two hours back,' said Riyaaz.

'We slept for 4 hours?' asked Feroz

'Well, almost,' remarked Riya.

All of them walked back to the Concurrence room. Everybody was still there. They were all discussing very quietly. When they saw Firan and Feroz they stopped talking and looked at them. Sir asked them to sit, and they both sat down.

'Hope you are not feeling too tired?' Sir said politely

'I am,' replied Firan, 'At least you could have warned us about this decontamination.'

'It slipped my mind to inform you that this could happen. You did not mention about the odour. Any smell can contaminate you and contaminate our environment.'

'But then you will also need to be decontaminated.' Feroz said quickly

'Oh! No, as soon as I met you I popped my safety medicine, which all of us carry at all times.'

'If everybody has the pill then what is need for decontaminating us,' retorted Firan.

'We have to safe guard our environment, Firan, you are very argumentative.'

'I am not; I just want to know about things, I can't go on blindly accepting everything you say.'

'Can you now remove our handcuffs?' asked Feroz.

'No, it remains till the situation is dealt with.' replied Aman'

If they can play games we can too,' whispered Firan to Feroz.

'What?' he asked, 'do you have in mind, another stupid idea?'

'At least I have some idea, you have none,' she replied and then added, 'listen, I didn't force you to join me, seems like you have forgotten all about your curiosity.'

She was all charged up. She turned towards all the Nouses who were now sitting in front of them and not alongside. She said, 'We will not tell you anything unless you remove our handcuffs.'

All the Nouses looked at each other. Aman stood up and came towards both of them and removed their handcuffs.

Somehow certain things these Nouses could do without talking to each other. *Certain actions that they made were almost as if by telepathy...* felt Firan. She also noticed that they never disagreed with each other.

Firan was sure they would remove their handcuff, if she put this condition, because she felt that they really wanted the information that they both could provide. This zone of theirs had been like a fortress to them, where no one could enter and exit without their permission. And their arrival had shaken them, indicating that somehow somebody had got access into their zone. This could mean that either there was somebody who was leaking information out, or somebody or something had penetrated their zone without permit.

What was this zone all about? Who were all these people who lived here and why was it created and how was it done? Somehow she had to glean all this information from them.

Meanwhile Feroz was thinking on completely different lines. *I have to get away from here and try to find a way back from all this madness. The first instant I step out of this building I have to run I will run not towards Sir's house but in the opposite direction. I hope Firan will run behind me, we would have to be very fast.*

His 400m track event seemed as if it had happened ages ago. He missed his friends and family.

'Tell us about the shadow that you both saw, can you tell something more about it?' asked Naga.

'You tell us why you are interested in it. What is this place?' said Firan.

Feroz understood what she was trying to do. Maybe once they get some information about this place they could try and get out of here.

Suddenly all of them got up and left the room. Only Sir and both of them were left.

23
Science Lesson

'It's getting late; we need to get back home, we will continue the meeting in tomorrow's session,' informed Sir and he went towards the opening of the room, Feroz followed.

He had to stop at the top of the step to brace against the bright light. As expected his eyes started watering. It wasn't before reaching the bottom of the stairs that they realized that Firan was not with them. Sir looked towards the opening, seeing that she was not in sight he started to go up the steps again.

'I'll check,' Feroz said and he ran up the step and into the Concurrence's oval room. Sir also followed.

They found that Firan was still sitting with no intention of following them.

'I'll not leave this room unless I get a few answers from you,' she said.

Feroz looked at her - annoyed, they could always find out little by little. *Why antagonize these people?* Sir however sat down opposite Firan

'Ask.'

Feroz also sat down

'What is this Zone all about?'

'Let me begin at the beginning,' he paused 'sometime in the 1980s a group of scientist and environmentalists came to the conclusion that human activity was making the earth a warmer place. Do you know about green house effect, global warming... Ozone depletion?' asked Sir

Both of them looked at each other, they knew that these were hot topics these days.

When they didn't volunteer to say anything Sir continued.

'Due to human generated emission of gases like Methane, Chlorofluorocarbon, carbon dioxide etc the atmosphere is showing signs of natural greenhouse effect. Err... At least do you remember what greenhouse effect is'

'It has something to do with .... Plants in a glass house... they grow......' Firan's voice trailed searching for the correct explanation ... err ....'

'You should really pay some attention in class' reprimanded Sir and added 'A greenhouse is a building with glass walls and roof; the glass allows sunlight to enter and traps it, it is ideal for the cultivation and exhibition of plants under controlled conditions.' He paused.

'Greenhouse effect is the warming that results when solar radiation is trapped by the atmosphere. This is caused by atmospheric gases that allow sunshine to pass through but do not allow the heat that is radiated back from the warmed surface of the earth to disburse...'

It made a lot of sense to both of them now, than when they had heard him explain the same topic in class. Seeing their expression, Sir continued

'In other words the atmosphere is able to transmit the visible light to the Earth's surface; however the presence of these gases is not allowing the transmission of infrared radiations back into the atmosphere, so the earth is becoming warmer,' He stopped and asked

'Are you following what I am trying to say...? I am trying to keep it simple.'

'Yes,' they replied in unison.

'The people you see in this Zone, all of them without exception, strongly believe that the humans are living indiscriminately and will have to pay a heavy price for it.'

'Pay a price ...how?' interrupted Firan.

'Like ... for instant the indiscriminate and abusive living might lead to a drastic change in climate, we may face extreme climate, I don't know exactly whether it will be too cold, too hot, earthquakes, tsunami, tornado .....basically the fury of nature. I think you can see some signs of it already, Excessive and bizarre rains in some part of the world; severe and early onset of winters...and this is only the beginning of the doom... there is a limit to how much the Earth can tolerate. The rate at which humans are at it, I think they are going to get wiped out...extinction of human race.'

'So.......' prompted Feroz

'So we have formed a team and we have created this Zone. It is back to basics here. We do not use anything that might hinder the atmosphere. We live consciously. We live like how we are supposed to live; we value everything...no extravagance, no misuse. We will make ourselves safe.' Sir said confidently.

'How was this Zone created? Asked Feroz

'I can't reveal that to you. It is a secret. Which reminds me might need to do a medical examination of your eyes. This zone cannot be seen by normal eyes.

The last statement terrified both of them. *Did knowing all this information put them in jeopardy? Were they better off not knowing all this? Will it now become even more difficult to leave this Zone?*

These thoughts went back and forth in their minds. They sat quietly for sometime.

A little later, Sir said looking at Firan, 'I know the burning question would be why you need your eyes to be examined. I will answer all your questions let us head home first, ok?'

Firan nodded and stood up; all of them trooped out and headed back to Sir's house without talking.

The brightness blinded them again and they felt the strain in their eyes again. The strain now infused into their tired body and they lagged behind a good distance from the striding Sir. They felt drained more and more with each step.

A strange sound like a rumble stopped Sir in his track. He looked back. Both the children also stopped. Then Sir started walking again, looking up and examining the sky at the same time. He beckoned them to hurry up. Another rumble emanated from nowhere. Sir stopped and turned towards them, they ran towards him. Sir looked up again; it was amazing how he could look up into such brightness without even squinting or showing any discomfort while they could hardly even lift their eyes off the ground. He searched the sky.

'Did you hear anything?' Sir asked the children.

'There was a sort of a rumble,' responded Feroz.

'Strange, very strange,' mumbled Sir, 'has never happened before...lets hurry,' he added.

They quickened their pace.

'What's that?' said Sir as he looked ahead.

'What?' asked Firan covering her eyes with her hands and trying to see through the gaps in her fingers.

A group of Nouses were huddled together way ahead. Sir started running towards the group and both of them followed suit not wanting to be left behind.

They reached the gathering. Firan could recognize Riya, Riyaaz, Aman, Naga and Nina from the fifteen of them that were there. Sir asked

'What's going on?'

'Oh! Batra, good you are here with Feroz and Firan'

They parted and showed an opening on the ground that was definitely the beginning of a tunnel.

'We found it,' said Riyaaz.

'Did you come from here?' asked one Nous, with a really hairy face, looking at Firan.

'No, not from here, but we did come from a tunnel like this, it was on the other side.'

'It is the same one; it's a wandering tunnel Nouses. We know who has breached our Zone now,' said the same hairy face Nous.

'Who?' asked Naga.

'Is it Yapra?' asked Sir.

'Yep,' said the hairy face.

'Manav, are you sure? Asked Aman

'Yes I am, Yapra has been working extensively with the birds and animals. He says he is experimenting with animal sense. I heard people on the other side talking about some strange behaviour by a pack of dogs in B2 area. Yapra also suspects that some of us are on to something. He is curious to know what we are doing, the other day he followed me for quite sometime,' Manav explained.

The name Yapra jolted Feroz and Firan. Everything came back to them in a rush. Realization dawned on them.

Was this part of the experiment he was talking about? Had he mesmerized them into coming here? They simultaneously felt woozy, this was beyond their control. What did he want from them?

Suddenly all the Nouses had become quiet. Firan was quite sure they were now talking telepathically. All of them were looking at the tunnel as if somebody was going to emerge from it and sure enough Yapra crawled out.

He did not cover his eyes as they had. He seemed to be able to see easily just like the Nouses. Riya and Riyaaz snapped the handcuffs on Yapra as soon as he stood up. It seemed that they were responsible for the security of the Zone. They still had the bags across their shoulders. Yapra looked around, his eyes widened when he saw the barren surroundings. He looked at the children before he was pulled and taken away.

24
Emergency

'We declare emergency. There will be a meeting tomorrow at 8AM instead of the usual 12' said Aman

Everybody went off in different direction.

Feroz and Firan followed Batra Sir. They walked silently each lost in their own thoughts. They were relieved to get inside Batra Sir's house. Sir made the same refreshing drink and told them he would be back soon and went outside again. Feroz and Firan were happy to be left alone. They wanted to discuss things now that Yapra had come into the scene. Both of them sat down on the thick rug and sipped their drink.

'I think we are a part of the experiment that Yapra was talking about,' Feroz stated.

'Yes, even I think so, but when did it start?'

'Let me see, that day at the shack when he said you were my partner... I didn't like it, and ... I'm sure even you didn't like it.'

'Yes... and then he said something like our minds were twin minds...'

'Ya and then he laughed... after that incident I didn't meet him or see him, did you?'

'No, I didn't, in fact I thought it was a mistake to have talked to him and promised all that... I dispelled the whole affair out of my mind.'

'Me too.'

'But you met him once before too didn't you?'

'Oh yes.' said Feroz and narrated the whole story to her. He suddenly said, 'In fact it was that very day you moved into the house!'

'Oh,'

Adrenaline was rushing through Feroz and some parts were beginning to make sense. All charged up he said, 'It is possible that Yapra wanted to use us to come to this world and get information for us. But since we didn't get back he landed up here himself.'

'You mean he made us visit the hideout together, he put idea into our mind to explore, and we know he created the tunnel...'

'Yes, I think it is possible, when we gave consent he could have hypnotized us to do his biddings.'

'But we were behaving so normally, we were doing routine things,' exclaimed Firan, 'did you feel anything?'

'I was wondering why we were getting paired up time and again, I mean... the seating... and for the science exhibition, you know... Bonty was doing very well in science so why me?'

Firan chewed her lips; it was difficult to comprehend how Yapra was leading them to this. She had started liking Feroz and she no longer felt that all boys were rude. When did this change happen?

Both of them started thinking the sequence of events and how exactly they started doing what Yapra wanted them to do. Their eyes felt very heavy and kept closing. Feroz slid down on the rug and mumbled,

'Why ...Sir want... eyes check...' and he fell asleep mid sentence. Firan did not hear the mumbling, she was already fast asleep.

Batra Sir returned quite late that night. He saw the children slumped and walked softly to the mattress and laid down. He had terrible news to tell these two children. All the Nouses had discussed and put in force some short term measures they had to take to control of the situation. Yapra had been given sedatives and forced to sleep.

They hated the intrusions into their pristine life, though they did go to the other side to carry on with their profession every day. They did not like the fact that their world had been discovered.

There were two reasons they kept their life on the other side going :- (a) they needed to be in touch with the activities on the other side. (b) They needed some components to make a material that they had discovered. They called it NEM, Non-energizing Material. It was with this material they had constructed all their buildings, clothes and other equipments. They returned back to Zone every evening, and during weekends and holidays they preferred to stay here. They had everything they required. Food was spiced up with chemicals that were essential for them and these were grown and prepared by the doctors in the zone itself.

Batra Sir started recollecting those early days when all this had started. All 24 of them lived in Park Lane... once upon a time. They knew each other as kids and used to meet now and then during society functions. They split and went different direction after completing school. All of them excelled in their chosen field, yet they felt unsatisfied. Though they were not very good friends or anything of that sort they kept in touch with each other. Slowly they gravitated towards each other and formed a group. They met every year at Park Lane and enjoyed each other's company.

Aman, a scientist, was deeply involved in studying metaphysics as a hobby. He loved to discuss how things came into existence and how the eyes perceive things. He would keep saying, 'everything is made of energy, everything. Nothing is solid, try to see differently. Take this table when you break it... what will you get? Small pieces and breaking them further will give the smallest particle? What if you break that too... ultimately there is only energy left'

His animated discussion on the subject piqued their interest and all of them started reading up articles and research paper on energy. The bond between them became stronger and stronger. Aman learnt to see energy and not the object. And he taught all of them to focus on seeing energy whenever they wanted too.

Batra Sir sighed those were exciting days. But those good days were short-lived. They started noticing rampant misuse of material things and the environment. Right in front of their eyes the world around them was turning into a night mare. They felt surprised that nobody was paying any heed.

They felt that they had to do something about it. They started making different things using their combined scientific knowledge. Things that would require less usage of natural resources, things that would be basic in its structure, things that wouldn't be easy to destroy, things if would get destroyed wouldn't leave behind any remnants.

They bought a large area of wasteland beyond the cantonment and tried all their experiments on plants in this area. Over a period of time the area was full of variety trees and shrubs. Some were too leafy, some twiny and some sticky.

One thing led to another and they discovered a material that couldn't be seen by normal people. They called it NEM. They built a building partly with this material and decided to live together in this building.

All of them had their own flats in this building. They spent more and more time together.

They became obsessed with their love for seeing energy. They started focusing more and more on energies rather than physical objects. This combined focus of theirs created a space that became visible to only them. They lost their ability to see physical object.

Manav, a doctor, was slow in this transformation process. When he realized from others that they had lost their ability to see physical object he got special lenses made for all of them to see physical objects. They had to wear these to see the normal physical world. That's how they moved between these two worlds. Each one of them had a room in the Concurrence. Every time they needed to go to the other side they had to collect their lenses and go to their room and wear the lenses. Immediately they would find themselves in their own flat in the building where they lived together on the other side. From there they could go anywhere. They would remove the lenses in their own flat and find themselves back in their room in Concurrence in the Zone.

People on the other side saw them coming from and going into through a thickly vegetated area. Some curious labourers followed Dr Manav once and saw him enter a partly dilapidated building. They went away disinterested.

That was how the zone was created; without the lenses it was visible to only them the way it did. In reality it could well be that it was milling with people and vehicles, or congested with buildings and roads. They would see concentration of energies at the spots where there was too much activity. They avoided going to such areas and remained in low energy area which in the real world would be a back lane or a deserted place.

For them it was vast expanse of land with only what they had constructed in their sight- peaceful, safe and unpolluted. They kept trying different experiments that might help them stay this way for a long time to come. The Zone was still in an evolving stage. Batra Sir had got special lenses made for his pets and brought them to the Zone as a part of an experiment and they found that the animals behaved peculiarly and seemed too confused to deal with it.

Batra Sir barely managed to sleep for a couple of hours and he was up and about by 6 A.M. He woke the children up and asked them to freshen up meanwhile he got the same drink ready and some sandwiches for breakfast. Then he dropped the bombshell.

'It has been decided that you cannot leave the Zone... ever.'

25
Oval Meeting

Yapra's grogginess started diminishing at around 6 A.M. but he did not move. His sixth sense told him that there was somebody in the room. He opened his eyes just a little and saw that the same people who had handcuffed him were huddled on two chairs looking away from him. They were talking to each other in very low tone. He looked around he saw a table with a half filled glass from which he had sipped some drink before dozing off.

When Yapra lost the sight of the children in his mind's eye he got worried because he did not expect this to happen. He immediately physically rushed to the spot where he lost them. He used his mind power to find them but he couldn't. The only way to find them was to create an identical situation. So with strong intention to find the place he hypnotized himself at the right time and went looking, he created a tunnel and went through it. He knew he was risking his life and his highly developed mind power may get lost in this other world, but there was no choice.

Now he looked at the two people in front of him and wondered how much of his mind power would be effective here. He knew that his trance had ended the moment he came to this world.

He began to check his mind power first he tried to self hypnotize himself, it did not work. He tried to listen to what the two were talking through his mind... he didn't have that power. He tried to form shadows and surprisingly he could do that quite easily. A nice shadow formed right in front of him he tried to move it ahead, it moved easily. He formed another very small shadow and moved it in front of the two to see if they would notice it. It was risky but he had to check. It was better to check now than when more people were around. The shadow was right in front of them but they continued to talk looking right through it. The shadow quickly melted away. Next he tried telekinesis, the power to move something by thinking about it without the application of physical force. He tried to attract the glass on a table it moved making just a little scrapping sound and he stopped it just in time as Riya and Riyaaz turned at that moment to check the source of the sound. Yapra pretended to stir and then sat up with a start as if he had just woken up.

'I am Riya, we will go to Oval Room for the meeting.' Said Riya seeing him stir and stood up adjusting her bag to lead the way.

Yapra looked into her eyes and tried to hypnotize her, short duration hypnotism was possible without consent. She did not get hypnotized. Then he tried the same on Riyaaz delaying by getting up rather slowly, even he did not get hypnotized, their minds were blocked. He realized that if they had learnt to use the power of mind then they might read his mind, he had to remember to keep it blank at all times.

Yapra followed her and behind him Riyaaz followed. They emerged from one of the rooms in the Concurrence itself. Yapra kept his mind blank, they passed several rooms each had a name; he looked at the names Naga, Nara, Nina... He wondered what all this meant suddenly he saw the name Riya written. He realized these were rooms that belonged to each of them. They passed the room called First Room, turned the corner and came to the front of the building and entered the oval room.

Everybody was already there; even Feroz and Firan were seated. Yapra was surprised to see that they were also handcuffed. Firan was looking at him with anger.

Aman spoke first and said, 'first things first, intruders are not allowed to go back. We cannot endanger our life's creation.'

'You cannot keep us prisoner here.' responded Yapra and then added, 'What sort of a place is this?'

'It is the place that you have been so curious about and gone to such lengths to know about. Now you are going to stay here forever. Batra will tell you all about this place.'

Feroz and Firan looked at each other, they were feeling very alarmed. After Batra Sir had declared the statement to them in the morning they had time to just get ready and come. They did not get a chance to talk to each other because Batra Sir did not allow them any privacy. Now Batra Sir was giving the same explanation about the Zone that he had given to them.

Firan glanced around the oval table; all of them aggressive. Aman looked most angry and it was clear that they meant every word when they said you cannot leave.

'Now that you know about the place and are going to remain here, let me introduce everybody. Batra Sir started from one end and called out their name and profession. They were not sitting in any order. So it was impossible to memorize the names and their profession. Firan and Feroz tried hard to register since they had met them earlier they were able to recognize a few names. Naga, Manav and Nina were doctors. Batra Sir, Riya and Riyaaz were teachers. Aman was a scientist and sitting next to him was also another scientist Dhanur. Three of the environmentalist were sitting together they were Samina, Puru and Chirag.

'In time you will know every one well,' remarked Aman with a smirk.

'How did you get to know about this place?' enquired Dhanur.

Yapra, who was using all his concentration to read at least one of the Nouses mind, contemplated what to tell. He didn't want to let them know about his mind powers. He suspected that they might already know a little about him so he could not lie blatantly.

'Batra's cat told me. I believe his pet Specter visited this world. So I knew the general area. My intention was to lead them,' he said nodding towards the children, 'to this place under a trance and see what happens, however things actually got out of control and I lost sight of them. I think the combination of my hypnotism on the children, and their intention to explore the area at the right time assisted in the formation of a tunnel that led them right here. '

Yapra paused and added, 'it took me a little time to figure out how it happened... the right time was the difficult part to guess...'

The children looked at each other feeling lost. Yapra then continued, 'I created the same situation by hypnotizing myself at the right time and found the tunnel and this place.'

All the Nouses started whispering to each other thinking that Yapra was done with his narration, however Yapra spoke again,

'When I entered the Zone I realized I was out of my trance and I was left in the same state in which you are. I mean I can see only energies no physical object' and started laughing in the similar manner in which he had laughed in the shack.

The children were terrified; here they were... stuck in a weird Zone with weird Nouses and a madman. Things couldn't get any worse.

After Yapra finished laughing, it became uncomfortably quiet. Feroz and Firan couldn't understand the last part of Yapra's statement.

All the Nouses were alarmed Yapra knew more than they had thought he would know. This was no ordinary inquisitive man. This was a highly intelligent and dangerous man.

The Nouses started discussing in very quite tones. Yapra watched them and again tried to read their mind, it was futile. Then he turned his attention on the kids maybe he could hear them. Sure enough he could clearly hear what they were talking about. They were talking about him and cursing him. Feroz was telling Firan that he would escape at the first chance. Yapra was glad to hear them because it meant that his ability was intact it was only that he couldn't hear the Nouses. Maybe he could put the children in a trance and make them do whatever he wanted them to. He had to escape and he needed help. So when Feroz looked his way he tried hypnotizing him there was no response he could not put him in trance. That power didn't work in the zone, which meant that he had to convince the children to find out more information about the Nouses.

Yapra had been so curious about this world that when he had read the cat's mind he had completely concentrated on how to get here. He regretted that he had not bothered to find out how to get out of here. This was going to cost him his freedom.

26
Meeting Contd

Feroz looked around at all the Nouses earlier they had seemed reasonable now they looked formidable. Firan started wondering what her parent's would do if she did not return. It would devastate them especially since Feroz would also not return.

Suddenly Samina asked in a shrill voice, 'What will they do here?'

'First we have to find out how they are able to see the Zone, which means a thorough eye examination.' said Manav.'

'I would like to study Yapra's brain functioning.' said Naga.

Aman turned towards Batra and said, 'remember the experiments we were doing with your pets, maybe we can try those on the kids here.' He looked excited.

'What a fantastic idea,' said Puru, 'we can try all our experiments on these people.'

'Yes, that should punish them for being so nosey.' Said Nina

'We weren't being nosey, me and Feroz, this Yapra made us do all this,' exclaimed Firan.

'Yes,' added Feroz, 'how can you punish us, we didn't do anything intentionally.'

'For starters you lied to your parents and sneaked out at night. That's your mistake,' replied Nina, 'you children have no respect for your elders. You don't deserve parents.'

'That's not true I love and respects my parents,' shouted Firan.

'Oh, just take them away, Riyaaz' said Aman, 'and you both get back here.' He said looking at Riya and Riyaaz.

Riya held Yapra and Riyaaz held them both and started walking fast. They turned the familiar corner and went towards the Decontam room.

'What again?' asked Feroz, when he didn't get a reply he added, 'oh for Yapra?'

'He was decontaminated last night itself. He slept all through' replied Riyaaz scornfully.

Feroz was thrown aback at the tone in which Riyaaz had replied. They were led beyond the Decontam room and passed all the rooms that Yapra had seen on the way to the oval room. Finally they were taken to the same room where Yapra had woken up. They were left in the room and Riya and Riyaaz locked the room from outside.

'Why are they being so rude?' asked Feroz

'They are not in their correct senses,' replied Yapra

'I was not asking you,' retorted Feroz, he almost said as if you are in your right senses, but he stopped.

Yapra knew what Feroz was thinking and did not blame him. He knew at times he himself was eccentric. He smiled instead.

Feroz looked at Firan. She was very quiet after that outburst.

'You have a lot of explaining to do,' said Feroz looking at Yapra, 'why did you use us like this?'

'I told you and you had agreed you can't blame me.'

'But why us? Is there any particular reason?'

'Well, children are more susceptible to hypnosis. They respond well to the directions. I chose you both because you both have the tendency to get totally absorbed in fantasy. I had been observing you for quite sometime Feroz and you were perfect.' He paused and stared intensely into Feroz's eyes and continued his narration,

'But when I made the mynah carrying your mother's shadow happen your mind wouldn't accept it. You made yourself believe that you were dreaming or something. Your mind needed a partner to believe in your fantasies. That's when Firan entered, you were meant to be friends, so like minded and all.

He then stole a glace at Firan. She looked back at him fascinated with the story.

'Unfortunately it didn't happen as quickly as I wanted it to...so I just aided the process by throwing you both together in various events. And then it happened. After that everything was easy.' He smiled

None of them returned the smile.

'Which part were we doing in a trance and which part was reality?' Firan finally spoke.

'Its difficult to segregate like that, the goal of the trance was to make you both go together someplace away from people's eyes and make you enter this world. I thought I would follow you in my mind's eye but I lost sight.'

He looked at their distressed faces and said, 'I know we are in a spot now,' He smiled nervously

Firan was ready to burst into tears; all this was clearly getting out of hand. More than anything the statement that Nina had made was pricking her mind like thorns.

'Why didn't you find out the way out of here from the cat?' asked Feroz

'Ahh... Yes the cat... It really liked you both didn't it? It especially liked your garden, once when it was supposed to come to me, it preferred loitering in your garden Feroz... under your sight,' he paused, smiled and continued, 'I had to distract it by accepting a blank call to you.' Yapra winked

Feroz shook his head in disbelief, behind all the weird happenings that occurred in his life there seemed to be only one person behind it. It was Yapra!

'I wonder why the cat was attracted to you both,' mumbled Yapra.

This brought Feroz back to the question he had asked. He asked again, 'Why didn't you find out the way out of here from the cat?'

'I was so intent about getting here, I had no intention to come here myself, so I guess I thought it unimportant. A mistake...'

'Why did you come here,' asked Firan suddenly

'Why? To get you out of course, I know you think the worst of me but I wanted to get you back.' He looked at them and asked 'Did you both find anything about getting out of here?

Both the kids looked sheepish. Even they had not managed to find out how to exit this place. They always got distracted by sudden turn in events. Yapra was not waiting for a response he already knew that they did not have the information.

Suddenly the door opened and Riya stomped in and dragged Firan out of the room. Feroz yelled, 'Where are you taking her?'

She did not reply.

Yapra and Feroz remained quiet and did not talk about anything. They were worried sick. Suddenly it seemed as if the Nouses were becoming more and more hostile. Earlier they talked quite freely explained everything, now they were extremely rude and refused to answer.

Firan returned after an hour or so. Her eyes were totally red and streaming. She refused to talk and slumped down in a corner. Then Feroz was taken away.

Yapra did not ask Firan anything he just used his mind power to read her thoughts and discovered that she was taken and her eyes were examined. He could even read the parts of her mind which had overheard the discussions between the Nouses. He heard them discussing how Firan's eye structure had somehow changed in the tunnel, now her eyes were capable of seeing only energies. And on top of that they were too weak and so kept watering.

Yapra resolved he had to get these children out of here. How could he correct their vision; he was at his wit's end. He paced back and forth in the room. The only way to know the way out was to ask one of the Nouses, but the bonds between all of them was very strong. Not even one of them would reveal it to him. He was sure even Batra Sir would not help the kids, especially because it was through his pets that they had got here in the first place. That thought made him realize that the cat or any of Batra's pet could provide him with that vital information. But he didn't know when and if ever Batra would get them here.

Feroz returned in the same state in which Firan had... eyes blood shot red, slightly puffed up and watering. It was now Yapra's turn. Yapra resisted trying to be led but this time Riya and Riyaaz had come and pulled him away easily. While grappling Yapra saw Riyaaz clutch his bag, there was something important in that bag that they always kept it with them. He wondered what it contained.

He followed them, observing them closely, every now and then they would adjust the strap and slide their hands along the bag. Out on the corridor this time they took the other direction to the Decontam room. Again there were some names in some rooms. They went into the fifth room that said I Room. Riya and Riyaaz left the room after leaving him inside. The handcuffs were not removed.

Manav and Dhanur were sitting and talking with each other. Yapra was led to a bed and made to lie down. Some eye drops were put into his eyes by Dhanur.

Yapra started thinking... *the Eyes seem to be very important to these Nouses. Why were they getting their eyes checked?* Slowly his thought process led him to the obvious reason and Yapra smiled.

27
Action

Throughout the time Yapra's eyes were getting checked his mind was working at double speed. The Nouses were surprised that the kids and he could see their world. This meant that it had to do something with the way their eyes worked. When he had entered the Zone he had seen the concentration of energies at some places, though he had not given it much thought. Now he realized that the energies had something to do with this.

He wondered what could have changed their structure of eyes to be able to see what the Nouses were seeing. Whenever they asked him to open his eyes and look into different machines he looked all around. He noticed a small door in the room and on it was written Lens Trials.

Did they require lenses to see this world while the children and he did not? Was that it?

He looked deeply into Manav and Dhanur's eyes while his eyes were getting examined. They were not wearing any lens.

Some more drops were put in his eyes and again he was made to lie down. He heard Dhanur tell Manav

'After 15 minutes.'

Yapra opened his eyes a little to see what was happening. Dhanur was heading towards the Lens Trial room and Manav was settling down into a chair and then he closed his eyes. Yapra quickly glanced all around again, the machines, the various bottles and instruments. Right next to the bed on the head side was a side table with vials of various drops. His eyes opened wide when he saw one small bottle marked sedative. He had to somehow take it...he inched his body to the corner on the bed, and glanced at Manav. Manav was completely still. Yapra moved his handcuffed hands towards the bottle; it was just a few millimetres away from his reach. He concentrated hard with all his mind power and the bottle moved noiselessly towards his outstretched fingers. He grabbed it and slid back into his original position. He worked the bottle into his pockets and hoped that it was not bulging out. He closed his eyes and lay motionless

He had no idea what he was going to do with it, but knew that it was a useful thing to have under the circumstances...

Manav opened his eyes and came towards Yapra and bent over him and opened his eye lids with his thumb and forefinger. He then called out to Dhanur,

'He is ready.'

They again checked his eyes with the help of a machine.

Dhanur was impressed with Yapra's eyes and blurted out

'You have very strong eyes.'

Yapra needed an excuse to talk and so immediately said

'Is it? I think my right eye is weaker than my left.'

'Let me see,' said Dhanur

After some examination, he said, 'May be, just a wee bit.'

'Can you let me try a few lenses,' asked Yapra

'No, we don't yet make lenses here.'

'But that Lens trial room...' Yapra started to say,

'That is none of your business...Riya Riyaaz we are done' he yelled out abruptly as if he had talked too much.

On the way back Yapra walked rather slowly trying to think of something to say and make some conversation.

'My eyes are hurting with all the drops that were put in,' he said. 'I feel they are swollen too,' he added, getting no reply he further asked, 'How long before it will be back to normal.'

None of them replied.

They took him back to the room and left him.

'At least take our handcuffs out,' he yelled at the closing doors.

Both the kids looked at him and went back to sitting with their heads down. They had not talked to each other at all.

'Ok, both of you, I have some good news, look at this,' he said and took out the bottle.

Both of them looked up and saw the bottle and Feroz asked, 'What will we do with it?'

'I don't know! Something will come up... try to think of a plan ... anything...'

Both of them were not feeling optimistic about the situation. Just then the door opened and Riyaaz brought a jug of that drink and Riya brought three glasses on a tray and left it on the table. Then they went out. The same lemony aroma spread quickly in the room.

'I am fed up of this smell and the drink,' complained Firan, 'I'm not going to have it.'

'It is a strange drink, one glass and you feel as if you have had a meal.' Remarked Feroz

Yapra picked it up and opened the jug, looked inside and smelt it.

It was a slightly yellowish in colour and quite clear.

'I had this drink last night and then slept like...,' and he stopped

Both the kids looked expectantly at him. Before he could say anything there was a sound on the door. Yapra quickly took the jug and started pouring the drink into the glasses. Riyaaz peered in and saw that they had not started drinking.

'Please drink up,' he said and went out.

Yapra looked at the children

'Just play along with whatever I say or do,' he said in a low tone.

He took out the bottle from his pocket and opened it and poured the content into two of the glasses filled with the drink. The third glass had the drink only which he kept at the edge of the table near him.

Riya and Riyaaz returned after some time to take the things away and found that they had not had the drink.

'Why aren't you drinking? Do you want to go hungry till we prepare your meal? Asked Riya

Yapra picked up the single glass at the corner of the table, and pointed with his head to the children to pick up the other two glasses. Firan and Feroz hesitated, but picked them up after a few seconds.

Feroz rubbed his nose thinking, *is he going to sedate us and somehow escape alone?*

Yapra brought the drink to his lips and stopped and suddenly shouted, 'Don't drink!'

The children opened their eyes and stood still. Riya and Riyaaz lifted their eyebrows and rolled their eyes,

'What?' asked Riyaaz

'I know what you are trying to do here, you sedated me the last time I had this drink. Now you are trying to force us to drink this...I am sure you are getting us sedated so that you can perform your experiments on us. What do you think I'm an idiot? I won't fall for it again.' He turned towards the children and said, 'For your safety I forbid you to drink that. Put your glasses down.'

Again the children hesitatingly put the glasses down, they began to understand where all this was leading.

'What nonsense, if you don't want to drink... don't drink. We will take it away, why are you forbidding the children.' Said Riyaaz

'It's more than eight hours since they had anything at all. We want healthy people here, even for experiments.' Riya said smiling slyly

Feroz thought *how nasty Riya looked, how strange that he had thought there was no danger here. These Nouses had transformed into heartless freaks.*

'If you are so bothered then why don't you both have a glass of that drink, if nothing happens to you then we will also drink?' Yapra said

Riya and Riyaaz exchanged looks and shrugged her shoulder.

'I could do with a drink,' she said looking at the two glasses on the table and then at Riyaaz.

Riyaaz nodded and came forward picked both the glasses and gave one to Riya. Both of them gulped it down.

'See? It's safe. Now you can have it,' said Riyaaz.

'Come drink,' said Riya looking at Yapra with the drink in his hand.

Yapra sipped a little wondering in how much time the sedative would start to affect. He didn't want them to go out of this room and faint somewhere outside.

He sipped as slowly as possible to gain time.

28
Un-Zoned

He watched as Riya came forward and put the glass down on the table. She proceeded to fill it up. Riyaaz came and put his glass down on the table but held the glass tightly before leaving it down. Riya stopped when the glass was half filled. She looked at Yapra and the jug slipped from her hand and she crashed on the floor with the jug. Riyaaz also fell down after a few seconds.

The crashing of the jug and the thud of them landing on the floor sounded magnified to the three of them. They hoped that nobody was close by and heard it. Yapra whispered to Firan to close the door and he started unstrapping the bag from Riya's shoulder. He asked Feroz to remove Riyaaz's bag. It was difficult to do that with hand cuffed hands, but he managed. Firan peered out of the room and looked left and right, nobody was there.

'Let's get out, nobody is there.' She whispered, 'We won't get another chance.'

Yapra wanted to look inside the bags, but he felt Firan was right they had to get away from here. So he quickly strapped the bag across Feroz's shoulder and asked him to strap the other bag on his shoulder. All of them sneaked out. Feroz locked the door from out side. All of them hurried on... they knew their way out. They turned the corner and quickly down the stairs. Feroz led the way and instinctively turned towards the other side to the direction they had taken so far.

Even though their eyes were watering madly they were able to run faster than Yapra. Yapra was looking with interest at the surroundings. He could see concentration of energies at different spots. As they ran aimlessly looking for some place to hide They ran and ran and ran.

Yapra observed the various pattern of energy. It was mesmerizing to him. Suddenly he saw flashes of energy zipping ahead and he stopped.

'Not that direction lets go this way,' he said and away from that area.

'Look there some tall grasses there, shall we go there?' enquired Firan

They headed straight there and crawled on their fours and sat down catching their breath. Yapra looked at their wet eyes and wondered whether they could see the vibrating energy all around

'Can you see anything unusual all around,' he enquired.

'Like what?' asked Firan

'Some bluish, reddish haloes...?'

'No' they said together

'Did you see anything like that?' asked Feroz

'I can see energy all around us.'

They looked alarmed and opened their eyes and turned their head left and right they couldn't see anything like what Yapra was describing. Seeing them react the way they did he realized they could not see the energies.

'It's ok, let's check what's in the bags.'

Feroz quickly opened it. He was sure there would be some handcuffs in it. He was surprised to it was containing lens-cases, twelve cases to be precise. They were made of the same material with which the door tables, chairs in Sir's house were made of. He opened one there was nothing inside; he threw it and opened another. Empty, he opened another, empty again. He felt dejected and disappointed.

Yapra yelled out 'stop', a bit too late. He pulled his own bag and carefully looked inside. There were twelve lens cases in his bag too. He took one out and opened it carefully. Yes, he could see light blue and light green colours of energy. He was sure they contained lenses.

'These have lenses, look,' he said and leaned to show the children.

Both of them peered inside, *there was nothing! What was Yapra saying?*

'I know you can't see it neither can I, but I can see that there is something in it I mean I can see an energy field.' He paused and then continued, 'look I am going to try something I don't know what will happen, but it might be worth a try.'

'What are you going to do?' asked Feroz

Yapra retrieved the lens-cases that Feroz had thrown and put them back inside his bag.

'We have to wear these lenses and see what happens...' he paused to see their reaction.

Both of them kept a straight face but a million thoughts were rushing through their mind. *Energy... lenses... had Yapra lost his mind*

'Please I beg you,' he said judging the expression on their faces.

Both of them remained quiet and stood still, unable to decide.

Yapra took out one lens and called Firan to come forward. Firan looked at the fore finger that was supposed to be balancing a lens. She went ahead thinking that Yapra would discover that nothing was there when he would try putting it in her eyes. Yapra carefully inserted the lens.

'Can you see anything?' he asked

Firan shook her head,

'I cannot see anything through the lens eyes.'

'Oh?' remarked Yapra and then added 'Let's hold hands while we do this.'

He took hold of Firan's one hand, Feroz held the other. With the free hand Yapra inserted one lens into Feroz's eye then one into his own. Then he proceeded to put the lenses into the other eye on each of them.

The brightness suddenly vanished and it became pitch dark. Darker than dark. Nothing and nothing could be seen at all. Fear gripped their hearts again. They sat holding hands for a long time. Their whole body became numb. *What now?* They wondered.

Slowly and steadily all the numbness began to wear off from their bodies. Feroz was the first to realize it. He wriggled his fingers and Firan let go of his hand. She immediately turned towards him. It was still dark but not that pitch dark, not darker than dark. She could see him faintly.

Feroz stretched his body straight and turned his head left and right. He let go of Yapra's hand. They peered into the darkness. Looked left and right, there was nobody around. It looked like they were in a vast land of emptiness. There was nothing, not even a stone, or a bush.

'Where is all the grass?' Firan whispered again.

'Dunno,' Feroz whispered back.

Slowly he turned around, he could see nobody around. Firan also looked around, no one was in sight. It was so quiet; it was unnerving. *What happened to the Zone?*

'Are we in the tunnel?' whispered Firan.

'No,' whispered Yapra.

'Why are you whispering?' It's scary when you whisper,' whispered Feroz.

'It's so quiet,' Firan whispered back.

'Come on,' said Feroz in his normal voice.

It did sound loud, however he continued 'Hello, anybody there?'

A dog barked and all of them nearly jumped out of their skin. They stood still. Yapra scanned the horizon. Firan looked in the direction from where the dog had barked. There were some distant faint lights.

'Are we on the other side?' asked Firan.

'Let us walk and see,' replied Yapra.

They started walking towards the faint light. Their eyes totally focused on the distant light. They walked for about a minute and they started noticing outlines of several buildings and dwellings. A few steps forward and sounds of cars, buses and other vehicles overwhelmed them. All of them stopped and looked left and right, there were buildings everywhere. People were walking, talking and going about their business.

'Huh?' remarked Firan

And she turned around to see the spot where they had stood rooted a few minutes back. Feroz also turned back instinctively and wondered, *why didn't I see all this from that spot?*

They twirled around again, all they could see were buildings, shops, road and vehicles. There was no empty ground or anything like that. It was confusing, puzzling and unbelievable.

'What happened? Where did we come from?' said an exasperated Firan.

She looked at her watch it was showing 9.25. Obviously 9.25 p.m.

Feroz also looked at his watch; it was 9.25 in his watch too.

Yapra looked around once more and murmured 'This place is familiar.'

'Ah I know this is Kirby Place. It is close to our colony! No more than half an hour's walk' said Feroz

'Really, come on then lets go.' said Firan.

They started walking fast. The noise, the crowd and smell of the place overwhelmed their senses. They felt a burning sensation run through their nose and into their throat. They felt dizzy, but did not slacken their pace. Soon the familiar site of their colony sent a feeling of joy and relief in them.

Firan suddenly stopped and said, 'what will we tell them?'

'The truth' said Feroz without stopping

'Will they believe us?' she asked jogging beside him

'I don't care whether they believe us or not. I am telling the truth.' He said and started running.

She followed him and Yapra also ran along with them.

When they neared Firan's house they saw a crowd near the gate. There was a police jeep with its light on.

The three of them stopped and looked at each other. Firan gave a confused look; Feroz felt a strange protective feeling surge for her through him. He looked at her and said, 'just tell the truth, ok?

She nodded and said, 'let's go.' And they jogged towards the crowd. Few policemen were standing here and there. Their parents were huddled together. Other neighbours were also there. Ajay and Bonty's parents were also there. They had found the bags in the hide out. They felt saddened to think that these two had decided to run away.

Everybody turned when they heard the sound of running feet. The adults couldn't understand and there was confusion everywhere. *Why were their kids in handcuff and who was this strange man.* Firan rushed to her mother and leaned on her. Mr. Shah rushed to Feroz and hugged him tightly. Tears rolled down the mothers' eyes.

Police rounded up everybody and asked everyone to assemble in the garden. The inspector told everyone to be quiet. They wanted to talk to the children to find out what action needed to be taken.

'First let me just ask one question? Were you kidnapped?' Inspector asked.

'No,' said both in unison.

They both narrated their adventure truthfully. From the expression of the adults they could make out that what they were telling was sounding bizarre and ridiculous. When they finished their story there was silence.

Yapra remained quiet throughout. He knew he was guilty. He was happy that the children did not make a villain out of him. The inspector took Yapra away after informing the parents that they would need to take the children to meet with some officials in the morning.

The crowd dispersed, some believed them, and some did not. Ajay and Bonty's parents hugged both of them and said that they were glad that both of them were safe. Firan, Feroz and their parents stood watching them leave.

Feroz turned and asked

'Do you believe us?'

'I believe you' said his Mom. 'Feroz you were born at 9.25pm,' and she turned towards Firan's Mom

'So were you,' said Firan's Mom.

This was news to both of them. It made sense that both their watches showed 9.25 and not some other time. Other than that ...they had no answers to the how, why and what....

Feroz and Firan said goodbye to each other and went to their respective houses.

Epilogue

All three of them were questioned several times after the incident. A lot of examination was done over next few months. The lenses that they had worn seemed to have fused with their eyes and were not discernable at all. Many officials and scientists talked to them. They were asked to narrate the whole incident again and the whole narrative was recorded.

Yapra joined the Indian Scientific Research team. They were analyzing the lenses that they were able to bring in those bags. He lost many of his earlier abilities. He was convinced that it would come back to him with time. He tried creating the tunnel but it never appeared.

Yapra and the other scientists walked through the growth several times and each time they reached the back lane of Arjun Vihar. The bridge, the tunnel, the lush growth, the thick vegetation was never found.

Some samples of the few trees around the hideout were taken and some tests were conducted on them.

When the results came in, it was found that the trees were unusually healthy; the leaves had some deposits of chemicals not usually found in plants.

Life for Firan and Feroz changed. Both of them shared a special bond with each other. In school they were treated royally for a few days. They narrated their adventure several times. Everybody wanted to be friends with them.

Batra Sir did not return to their school. A new science teacher arrived after a gap of two weeks. Everybody forgot about Batra Sir's idiosyncrasies and missed him, their 'Prof Moody'.

Just for your information – None of the Nouses returned to work.